A Quiet Sound

Monika Brandenburg

contents

Broken Clocks

S he was bored as the teacher, Mrs. Smith, continued her never-ending lecture while she tapped her pencil against the wooden desk. Until she heard the day's final bell ring loudly, the woman hummed along to her music through her airpods.

Before class ended, professor Mrs. Smith told the students crammed into her college classroom, "and before we end this class I just would like to let y'all know that the essay is due tomorrow, so make sure that's turned in by midnight, or that ass is grass."

Chianti made her way out of the classroom and into the corridor, making her way to the parking lot where her matte brown stiletto was neatly parked. "I'm letting y'all know this now, push me and we fightin," she said.

The sound of her car's engine roaring and Jay Z's 4:44 album playing made her heart grin. She sighed gently as she got ready, got in her car, and started it. She then pulled out of her parking spot and drove home as the bass from the record beat banged threw her car.

"And where the fuck have you been at?!" Dominique was waiting for his fiancée to arrive home when the words seethed from his throat as he stood by the front entrance.

Chianti was not like most women in relationships who return home to a 'hello baby' or 'how was your day?' instead, she spent more time yelling and shouting at Dominique.

At school, Dominique, where else would I be? Her sentence was interrupted by a swift smack to the cheek; ordinarily, she would take it and leave the room before things got worse. However, today marked the end of their relationship, which was a toxic ball of slime.

I'm tried, my nigga, if you put your fuckin' hands on me! I'm out getting my fuckin' education and trying to create something of myself while you're sitting on your broke ass, but you always want to think I'm doing something wrong. She shouted, her fists flailing madly, her chest heaving from the strain of her breathing.

He responded by getting in her face and yelling, "broken?!, who broke bitch?!," which caused her to turn her head to the side and push him away with her forearm.

She said, "Mane watch out." stepping into the kitchen, putting her bag of supplies down, and obtaining a drink of water. With him, she was exhausted both mentally and physically, which was pointless.

"nah bitch watchu say?!" She turned to face Dominique, whose hot breath smacked her in the face as she nearly saw the redness in his eyes. Her back slammed into the kitchen wall.

"What the fuck is going on in hea!" Dominique let her go without delay while turning to look behind him when he heard chianti's mother Kimberly's voice.

Seeing her mother gaze at her with such concern was like a switch being switched in her brain. Her eyes were opened to the severity of the abuse she was going through.

"Get out. Dominique glanced at her in disbelief as she spoke calmly to him. He hadn't anticipated her actually ejecting him from her home. He had never taken her repeated threats to evict him seriously, but something about her tone and expression told him otherwise. She was completely serious.

You heard me: "Wha-" "Get the fuck out, nigga! You have the gall to insult me despite the fact that you haven't paid a single bill in this bitch? Get the fuck out of here, not nomo. While her mother stood by silently, she demanded, interrupting his thought with a direct look in his eyes.

He stood there for a few more silent seconds with his teeth tightened until he muttered a short "ight" and stormed out, slamming the door behind him.

Her mother asked her with sympathetic eyes, "chi baby, what was that? " as she shook her head and continued to fill her glass with water from the glass water pitcher.

Nothing, just know that this time I'm finished with him. Though she didn't truly believe she was through, her mother softly grinned at her daughter and said, "I'm ready to move on." She was afterwards reminded to pray that her daughter was being sincere.

As she slowly but steadily opened her hooded eyes and peered around the room without moving an inch, the alarm on her iPhone resounded throughout the room.

Chianti stood up and slipped her French-tip polished toe-nails into her white slippers after turning to her side to glance behind her and sighing with pleasure when she saw no evidence of Dominique next to her.

She said, "Alexa, play as soon as I get home by Faith Evans on shuffle," as she stretched. After a brief period of silence, Faith's voice rang from the Alexa speaker.

Yes, your love is fantastic, and I hope I never lose you.

I'll make it up to you as soon as I come home, sweetie. sweetie, I'll do what I have to.

I'll make it up to you right away when I get home, baby; I'll do what needs to be done.

She started her daily routine by squeezing a significant amount of body wash into her washcloth and turning on the shower at the highest temperature it would go.

This was one of the few times she had a tranquil morning without anyone bugging her about taking too long to shower or putting too much effort into her appearance. She was determined to get used to this, no doubt about it.

Chianti left her apartment after locking the door behind her and grabbing her keys off the counter. She and her best friend Emiko had made the spontaneous decision to have a much-needed girls' day today, which Chianti quickly agreed to because she needed a day off from Dominique drama and school.

Any moment, Any location By Janet Jackson was playing through the car speakers as she travelled to the Brookfields outlet mall through the streets of New York.

Emiko was waiting for her in the mall as she entered as she leaned over the steering wheel in search of parking, which was practically difficult on a Saturday. After finding one, she locked her car and got out.

She asked, slipping her keys inside her purse so she wouldn't lose them, "aight watchu' tryna go into first?

Chianti nodded in agreement as Emiko said, "Well I was thinkin' we could eat sumthin' first, then we could do a lil retail therapy."

"Okay, what do you have a taste for?"

Emiko complained in a hungry way, "I was thinking some Chick-fil-a," as Chianti looked at her.

"You got money for Chick-fil-A?" Emiko slapped her lips in response to Chianti's joke, which she did not find amusing in the slightest.

When shopping with Chianti, Emiko was infamous for 'forgetting' her money and believing she would pay. She had no issues indulging her pals, but she struggled with feeling manipulated. which Emiko was unmistakably attempting.

"Let's go, I actually do this time." Emiko muttered, hesitant to mention the joke despite her little embarrassment.

Chianti said, "Okay let's go, I have class at 4, so we've got a couple hours to shop," and then she followed Emiko to the food court.

They shopped and ate, but I'm skipping the mall. Okay ? Ok.

*

Chianti listened to her teacher rage about her husband's adultery as she sat in the back of the classroom, her mechanical pencil tapping lightly on the desk. When her phone gently rang in her pocket, she quickly grabbed it to check the notice.

When she realised it was a text from domnique, she said, "ew." The more she gazed at the two messages, the more her face tensed up.

Naturally, he began love bombing her right away, telling her how much he cared for her, how tired he was of being poisonous, and how he would make amends and be the greatest guy he could be for her. Bullshit typical of narcissists.

Then he began threatening her, claiming that if she didn't reply, things would get ugly. He threatened to come after her, break into her home, and beat her ass. She simply blocked him and gave herself a little reminder to change her locks as soon as possible.

Her teacher glared at her over her large, black specs and said, "No texting in class, Miss London," while Chianti nodded and slid her phone back into her Gucci purse.

When she turned around to face a very tall man she had never seen before, she felt a gap in her shoulder and a flood of perfume and marijuana odour filled her nostrils.

His hands were covered in a variety of tattoos, some large and others minor, the most obvious of which was 'Dave East' written on his fingers. He was much taller than Chianti, therefore it was obvious that he needed to participate in sports. He took very good care of his hygiene, as evidenced by his clear-polished fingernails, clean lips, and Carmax-covered lips. You could also tell that he had some sort of wealth from the jewellery that adorned his wrists and neck. an excellent one at that.

She discreetly grinned and nodded at him as he said, "Hey, I just wanted to come say wassap witchu' because I haven't seen you around campus at all."

He nodded, taking in the information she was prepared to tell him as she said, "I got transferred from another college, thus my fourth day here.

He grinned at her and she grinned back, saying, "Oh that's wassap' I'm a sophomore so I just thought it was because you were younger than me."

I'm Chianti, by the way, she said as she extended her hand to shake his. "I'm David, but people call me Dave or East because that shit so damn proper," he joked as he shook her hand.

Why the hell are you talking to this girl, bae? East's countenance shifted from happy to really displeased by the woman's presence as a high pitched, mildly unpleasant voice was heard from behind.

He responded, not even turning to face her, "she new here, making her feel welcome."

She rolled her eyes and shifted her weight from one thigh to the other, saying, "Yea okay."

Anyway, as I said before using my name key, I guess I'll see you around school, East concluded as Emily stood behind him, mugging Chianti, who replied unperturbed throughout the entire exchange, "aight fine, if you wanna talk to this mole r-" Chianti got out of her chair, making Emily flinch. Emily wasn't used to people approaching her, partly because she avoided confrontation with those she believed couldn't defend themselves. Chianti calmly said, "I'm telling you this now, get the fuck outta my face before I knock yo manly ass out," terrifying Emily who backed away from Her desk despite her unable to defend herself.

"If you hit me, I'm calling the police." She threatened, and Chianti shrugged, saying, "I don't give a fuck about the police. Emily continued to Mugg the two from the other side of the room as she rolled her eyes once again and left.

East attempted to lighten the mood by saying, "Aye sorry about ha' you badder than any molerat i Eva' seen," but he only significantly irritated Chianti more. He didn't say anything to him; he only started at him before grabbing her belongings and walking away.

The moment Dave saw his 'lover', who had folded her arms and was grinning, he shook his head and dragged his trainers across the room to meet her.

Are you done talking to that bi-"

"Man, stop talking so loud. How much longer must I date your ass? She rolled her eyes and laughed at him as he asked, "Man, until I get enough followers?" as she flipped her slightly knotted synthetic weave.

He sucked his teeth and waved her off. "Man, stop all that bullshit, you acting like I really wanna be with you ass," he said. "Oh I see, so you saw her now you imma rush to stop dating me."

She snarled, smiling slightly, "Keep talking shit and I'll send this video of you smoking to the basketball coach."

Due to her knowledge of David's fame as a professional athlete and the importance of basketball to him, Emily was able to blackmail him into dating her when she saw him smoking marijuana at a party. which was successful.

"Chill, why you doing this shit? " he asked, unable to see why someone would purposefully cause other people to be annoyed and depressed for their own gain.

She grinned at him, kissed his cheek, and said, "Blackmailing is my favourite thing to do." He vigorously whipped his cheek, acting like a young child who had just received a kiss from his grandma.

She turned to look at him behind her as he said, "that and illegal butt injections." "What was that?" she asked. Although she did nothing to alter the fact that her thighs didn't match at all, indicating that they were injections, she detested it when others brought up her injections.

He waved her off once more, saying, "Nothing mane," before she turned around and continued on her walk.

Still in love, and still in love, and still in love.

stunin' on ya old nigga

"**S**hould I just get one...fuck it, I'm grown, I do what I want" Before leaving the freezers holding ice cream, frozen fruits and veggies, etc., Chianti threw two ice cream items into the cart.

From behind her, she overheard a tease: "Chianti, Chianti, Chianti." She slowly moved her head to the right, where key was standing with his hands in his sweatpants pockets, and grinned as she recognised the voice.

David leaned over and peered into her cart, mostly finding junk food, as she sarcastically said, "Hello David," keeping a sneer on her face.

She grinned as she turned around and continued walking out of the frozen food department as east walked behind her, hot on her trail. "whatchu up in here gettin'" he asked, leading her to look around the grocery store carefully.

She spun around and gave him a 'nigga stop lying' look as she rushed up to him, saying, "woah woah, yo ass walk to damn fast, bout to flare up my asthma."

Oh, please. If you have asthma, it's probably due of that, she said, pointing at the neatly rolled backwood on his ear. He removed it from behind his ear and put it in his pocket while sucking his teeth.

"Man, this?" This exact moment? She shook her head slowly and walked towards the self-checkout as he quipped, "Helps my asthma.

"Boy I do don't have time for yo ass," she said, blushing slightly. "Then who's taking up yo time?" Key said, tipping his head to the side.

She added bluntly, "You need to be giving yours to yo gal. I chuckled a little at how quickly his smile disappeared when Emily was mentioned.

He handed her her phone, which she knew was in her back pocket, saying, "Anyway, imma see you lata' though, might just call you." Before she could finish, he left. She made the decision to leave things alone, bag her groceries, and head home.

Chianti dragged as she tossed goods in the back seat, deleting domnique's fresh text thread with the words "this nigga need to LEAVE ME ALONEEEE."

East shoved Emily off of him and back onto the coach as she attempted to push the camera into his face for an Instagram post. "Come onnnn let's take a picture for instagrammm, gim-mie a kiss," she said.

Upon hearing East's answer, Emily scrunched up her face in disgust. "Man move, don't nobody feel like having a camera pushed in their face every damn five seconds," she said.

She rolled her eyes, "mmtch, can you stop being a bitch." David tried his hardest to play the cards he was dealt, but he was at his wits' end. Despite the fact that he didn't really like her, he would never openly reject or insult her.

"Calm down, you bitch term. He made the threat because he was sick of her consistently degrading him and his manhood for fun and getting away with it because of her blackmailing. "I don't hit women, but I'll have my mom yo here in a second.

She responded with an aav threat, "nah cause I'll deadass leak this video," in an effort to sound cool.

Emily wasn't from the hood; her family was rather upper class. She was unable to fight. She never really needed to dig it out of the dirt, but she transformed herself because she wanted to be popular so badly. It's amazing how unaware individuals like her are of how fortunate they are.

"You know Emily, what? Leak the mothafuckin' video; doing all this extra work, stressing myself out, and ruining my own mental health just to keep it from getting out isn't worth it anymore; leak the mothafuckin' cueo; then get the fuck out. He snapped, which surprised Emily just a little.

Nevertheless, she took out her phone and texted the coach and the head of the basketball team the email that had been sitting in the seats for three months.

sent. good bye! And good luck with your basketball career, too. He was left sitting on the coach in the red-lit living room with his head in his hands after she slammed the front door of his apartment. He knew he had just bid his basketball career farewell. Nevertheless, he felt a little relieved to be free at last.

Since most of the students was either on their phones or sleeping, the reading teacher stood at the front of the room and ranted endlessly about how she shouldn't have eaten a hot dog for lunch the day before because she was ageing.

"pisttt," Chianti exclaimed, ignoring the boy's strange noises next to her. "pisttt, chi, chi, chianti!" she slapped her hand down on the desk and turned to look at the childishly smiling east.

She muttered, "What could you possibly want that darn bad?

" you. But that's not the topic we're discussing right now. Why didn't you text me yesterday? She smirked at his attempt to move beyond his initial reaction as he answered.

For the umpteenth time, she asked, "Don't you got a whole girlfriend?" She wasn't the kind to ruin a relationship, whether it was joyful or not. She had no duty to decide that. His expression changed when Emily was brought up.

"mmtch, look, that's not my girlfriend nomo', I can explain allat later if you text me," East said in an attempt to sway her into sending him a text.

She took a moment to consider her options before she finally smiled, flashing her dazzling teeth.

Okay, but could you text me instead? While maintaining his composure, East nodded, his mental muscles were strengthening three times over.

"All right class The teacher, Miss Robinson, shouted, "I'm giving you all a book to read. It's called 'the great Gastpy' I know y'all are going to enjoy it. She was one of the kindest senior citizens you would ever meet; she smelled like cocoa butter and vanilla, and it was obvious that she adored books and reading.

Chianti laughed as East muttered, "she always wants us to read something. Oh, I'm funny huh? " He winked and prodded her slightly. Before the bell rang and everyone started gathering their belongings and swarming the hallway, she muttered, "mmtch, boy bye," while he was looking her up and down and chewing his lip.

Before exiting into the crowded hallway, east winked at her and said, "ight, imma text you, you betta answer."

She blushed and walked in the opposite direction, east, towards her car, saying, "Whewww Chile."

Chianti giggled as Emiko pulled her head back to give her a clear view of her ass and said, "yo ass always eating sum," as she skipped to her always-full fridge. "Lemme go see what's in yo fockin fridge," she said. She stuck out her tongue and did a little twerking before heading to the refrigerator, saying, "You see where it's going anyways.

Chianti said, "Girl boo," as her phone rang to signal a text.

When she saw "east," her face curled into a smile instead of her usual grimace of loathing, thinking it was another bipolar text thread from domnique. As for Dora, I have put all of you to rest.

You were playing chess, baby, but this is checkers.

peace of mind

She was startled out of her slumber by the sound of her phone ringing. Whoever was on the other end of the phone didn't make her want to talk.

Without checking the caller id, she yelled, " what?! " at the person on the other end of the queue.

She heard David's voice on the other end of the phone, who seemed extremely sorry for what he had done, and her mouth slightly dropped as she heard him say, "well damn my bad, I just wanted to know if you were ready for our date."

She hastily kicked off the blankets and slid her feet into the slippers that were waiting for her by the door of her bed, saying, "Oh my bad, I didn't look at the caller id, I'm getting up now."

Let me go back a little bit. After David acquired Emily's number, he and Chianti spoke on the phone for hours as David described how he ended up with Emily. By the time they finished talking, Chianti was disgusted with the idea of Emily.

Then, after a brief period of getting to know one another, David proposed a date to her for Friday, which was three days ago. Now that David was taking her out today, they were both anxious and eager about the event.

Before saying farewell and Chianti entered the bathroom to get ready, he remarked, "alright mama, make sure you were something for outside."

Boys ll Men's song End of the Road was playing in her house as she crooned along to the lyrics. Her thoughts were racing a mile per minute, especially with the upcoming move out of her flat.

Though Dominique had been largely silent during the previous few days, she had been a little frightened even though she had never been scared. Because of her father's character and the way she was raised, she frequently witnessed the negative effects of enemies or people who pose a threat to you being silent.

The first date she had in a very long time, she nevertheless shrugged it aside so she could enjoy herself with David.

"So how are we liking the fit?" Chi inquired about her attire when she was on FaceTime with Emiko, who was energising her.

The ice is about to make me blind, yessss gorl! Chianti rolled her eyes at the remark as Emiko laughed, "Chileeee fuck saweetie you the REAL icy girl.

Chianti stated as they said their goodbyes and hung up, "ight, imma talk to you later David just texted me and said he's outside."

She gathered her belongings, locked the door to her house, and gritted her teeth in frustration as she noticed the man standing on his porch steps, appearing to be waiting for her to leave.

He wrinkled his face up and looked at her attire before she snapped," domnique what the fuck do yo ass want ".

"Nah, fuck allat where you're going, witcho tittes all out and shit! He grabbed her face and said, "You gon' need to change allat!," leading her to lean back against a porch corner.

I've got to tell you sh*t, buddy Ian. As she shoved him out of the way, she yelled, "Watch out." But as he drew her back by her wrist, her bracelets slightly scraped her skin.

He growled and dragged her in while attempting to kiss her, saying, "Nah to ass ain't going no fuckin where."

Meanwhile, David tapped his foot angrily while driving. "Mane imma just go in fuck it," he muttered as he waited outside her gated townhouses before he drove up to the gate and entered the code she had provided for him before driving in.

Since her residence was the sole fourth-floor apartment in the complex, he shut the car door and made the decision to approach it on foot.

Mr. Dominique I'm not good at br-. After Chianti's laboured voice, he heard a deeper, more male sound.

Chianti and the man then came into view as he observed him holding onto her neck tightly while she attempted to kick but seemed to lack the strength to do so.

"ayo!" David exclaimed, alerting domnique to his presence and slightly frightening him with his voice.

She fell while attempting to recover her breath because she was on the verge of going unconscious and he laughed, "I know yo hoe ass ain't call anybody.

How on earth could I have phoned someone when an ass was suffocating me, nigga? Before approaching David, who was waiting at the end of the driveway, she yelled and hurried over to him.

domnique waved her off and said, "Mane, I'm gone, keep the hoe," before putting back on his hood and heading to his car.

Watch that term, nigga: "Watch that hoe!" Before checking on Chi, East shouted out to him. Thankfully, she had no injuries, but the expression on her face made him want to slap Dominique. He refrained from telling Chianti that he was angry because he thought it would ruin the planned date.

"Man fuck that nigga, we'll deal with that lata but right now I wanna enjoy my time witchu, how about we just chill hea," he said, getting Chianti to nod as he picked her up and carried her inside the house. "Okay, imma cook a little sum fa you, show you chef east a little bit," he said, sitting her on the couch.

To get her attention, David approached her and knelt down to her level, saying, "Aye, wipe that frown off your face." He kissed her face and then grinned at how quickly her expression changed when he mentioned the Hennessy and marijuana. "I brought some Henny and weed everything gon be copasetic," he remarked.

"Girl, I'm hungry as he- oop, am I intruding on something?" Emiko entered using the key Chianti had provided her to find Chianti and Dave watching a movie together in bed with the lights dimmed.

I'm David, and it's wonderful to meet you. "Nah, you ain't. Emiko and David exchanged handshakes after David introduced himself and extended his hand for a shake.

Emiko shook David's hand and stated, "Emiko, Chianti FIRST and ONLY love." David giggled a little at emiko's snobbish attitude towards Chianti.

We're kind of in the middle of a date, so we'd appreciate it if you could leave, you met him now, Chianti said with a sarcastic grin as she escorted Emiko out of the house and shut the door before locking it.

Emiko said to herself, "mmtch, whatever I gotta betta shit to do anyway," before walking off the porch, hopping in her rental car, and driving to a very familiar person.

"But in truth, domnique wondered, what if she finds out? Emiko questioned while domnique rolled his eyes at her for lying and claiming she wasn't afraid of Chianti. "I'm not scared or anything, but I know that Chianti can box, I'm not tranna get fucked up plus me and you were fucking with each other while y'all together, that's a whole nother ballgame," Emiko replied.

domnique rolled a blunt while saying, "Mane that was in the past she ain't worried about me."

Emiko said, "but you worried about ha," but domnique could still hear her, which caused him to turn around and gaze at her.

"Whatchu talking about Emiko, fuck you heard?," domnique erupted as he positioned his hands on either side of her, essentially encasing her.

"Mane that bitch lying, but enough about her hoe ass, you know what to do," domnique smirked as he pulled down his boxers, causing his semi-hardon to spring free and cause emiko to smirk and get to her knees. "She told me you showed up to her house today and choked her," emiko revealed while domnique looked away sucking his teeth.

She was aware that Chianti would learn the truth soon enough, and that she would almost certainly lose her ass as a result. She didn't care or worry about it, though; instead, she was concerned for domnique and herself.

My peace of mind is in him.

How wonderful it is to be alive.

I GOTCHa man

The air in the classroom felt different to David , his mind was clouded at the mere thought of what was about to happen. On one side he was beating himself up for being to reckless knowing how much his basketball career meant to him but on the other hand he was pissed that Emily would do something to weird just to date him.

David wasn't a very shallow person and Emily was far from ugly and if she would've just spoke to David , got to know him , they could've been a actual couple.

" David Brewster " the teacher called his name out while all eyes shifted from there laptops to him David looked up at the teacher knowing exactly what she was calling him for seeing that she had just got off the phone.

" you needed in coaches office . " David sighed before nodding , getting up slowly from his desk and giving Chianti who sat right next to him , a kiss on the cheek before making his way out the classroom, he made eye contact with Emily who smirked at him and laughed loudly as he shook his head leaving the classroom and made his way the the gym

" you lucky I care about my education or i would stomp to ass threw this motherfuckin classroom floor " chianti to gritted asking Emily take away her smirk and quickly looks back to her laptop.

Meanwhile , david sat in the Coaches office as him and the coach stared at eachother for a couple seconds before the coach finally spoke

" first I wanna say goodmorning David I hope this news doesn't ruin you day , but we have received an anonymous video with visual representation of you smoking at a party and as you know smoking is prohibited when your on the basketball team so - yea I know " David said before getting up and leaving the office , not wanting to hear anything else he had to say to him he decided to ditch the rest of class and take a walk around campus.

Chianti stood in the middle of the hallway with her phone opened to her and David's text thread when she felt someone wrapped there arms around her waist slightly scaring her .

" who the fu-" she turned around ready to go off on whoever decided to grab her but her mug turned into a smile she saw David standing there Looking down on her.

" boy don't be sneakin up on me like that ! But are you okay ? I know how much basketball mean to you " she ask him , her hands holding onto his face as he smiled and shrugged.

" yea I'm straight. I mean it do suck that I can play no more but I'll be aight , but you wanna know what would cheer me up? " he smirked gripping her waist while she laughed looking away.

" what boy ? "

" lemme take you on a real date , like a movie theater " David suggested while shaking his head yes like he was eager to go to the movies

Chianti decided to go in the theatre and save there seats while David went and got them some treats from the con session stand , when he got to the front he saw a young lady that looked close to there age looking at him.

" hey welcome to amc what could I get you " she tried to say seductively making David slightly cringe but nonetheless he ignored it and started to order.

" uhh hi. Lemme get uhh two large coco cola slushies , and two, large popcorns with extra butter " he order making her nod her head and go make the order.

" uhh how about I get your number " she leaned over the counter as he grabbed the cup holders and the popcorns trying to show her flat chest threw her unbuttoned work shirt

David smirked before they exchanged numbers and he walked off into the theater , sitting next to Chianti was was deep into the movie.

" thank you " she smiled as he handed her the large popcorn and her slushee before her phone dinged from the text

Chianti looked around frantically while David watched her smirking at her face.

" you aight ? "

"naw I just got a werid ass text message from somebody, I think it's domnique weird ass " Chianti said making David bust out laughing.

" what ? " Chianti scrunched her eyes rows up seeing that she thought what she was saying wasn't funny.

" this girl at the con session stand was being all thirsty fa my number so I decided to give ya your number " David explained while still laughing which Chianti didn't find funny.

" mmtch , yo ass had me scared thought his crazy bass was bout to start something " she rolled her eyes while David shrugged.

David didn't see domnique scary in the slightest way. to him he was light work , but he still understood Chianti's concern with him showing up at her house and all.

" well when you wit me you don't have to worry about him aight ? " he used his index and middle finger to turn her head to look at him as she nodded and they shared a small kiss

" fuck you want emiko ? " domnique snapped , he was genuinely starting to get irritated by how clingy emiko was , he wanted a girl that would let him come and go when he pleased.

" why you acting like that ? Like you being rude for no damn reason " emiko said in a high pitched tone , she had literally just walked threw the door of his home and she was already being disrespectful. Usually he'd wait till she was good and comfortable until he started being rude.

"man i always act like this , fuck you acting like this new for ? And why tf you wearing that big ass sweater , you turning me off with that shit." domnique tilted his head to the side looking at her , she rolled her eyes and plopped down on the leather couch in his living room.

"nigga I'm wearing these because I'm pregnant you asshole ! " she yelled as he halted all movement and started at her for a second before shaking his head.

"welp guess you a single mom then huh ? " he laughed.

Tears built up in her eyes as she gathered her purse and keys before making her way to the door. She felt like he loved her and to find out that he didn't. Stung.

"fuck you domnique! Me and my baby gon be good always ! " she yelled before she slammed his front door before climbing into her vehicle and driving off.

"Bi-bitch recognize I got these thick thighs
And this pretty pussy that ya old man prides "

Breakin' Dishes

FOUR MONTHS LATER

"you wanna come ova to mines today?" David questioned as Chianti walked infront of him, her hips swayed with every step she took in the tightly fitted white sweatpants she wore.

"yessss, ouuuu I wonder how it looks" she replied thinking about how David's house would look since she'd never been, she only knew that he lived in the luxury apartment complex not far from her townhouse. David didn't seem like the type to have decor or anything other than the essentials; couch, bed, tv etc, so she was excited to see what his place looked like

"like a house" he said in a 'duh' tone while Chianti sucked her teeth, she had a love hate relationship with his sarcastic tones.

It had been four months since the movies and finding out the emiko was pregnant, Chianti was over the moon when she found out that she was having a god baby which ate more at emiko's conscience everytime she and Chianti went shopping for the baby. But it didn't make much a difference because she was still in sexual contact with domnique without Chianti knowing.

Chianti and David on the other hand , were doing amazing in the relationship they spent nearly everyday together with-er at school or at Chianti's place , and for the most part Emily had been quiet. Almost to quiet.

But other then that , they were both doing great , David wasn't even that hurt over his basketball career anymore , he was more focused on his grades and Chianti.

"oh and bring a bikini " David mentioned as him and Chianti walked towards her car, she stoped and turned around looking at him, confused about his request.

"for ? " she questioned.

"because I got a pool and I know ain't nobody gon be in there "David shrugged causing Chianti's jaw to drop.

"and you chose not to tell me why ?! Imma be over there everyday from now on ." she declared while David opened up her car door and helped her in before closing it as they talked there her opened car window.

"yea ight I wouldn't mind if you was there everyday anyway so "he shrugged , he truly enjoyed chiantis company , nothing was ever dull or boring when she was around. And that was one of the things he was find hisself to love about her.

" aight imma see you there " she kissed him before they exchanged goodbyes and she left to her home to back a spindanight bag.

" alright na show where the pool is ! " Chianti screamed as she smiled doing a happy dance while she stood in his living room , his house was ver manly yet homey at the same time , she liked it.

" wow , just using me for my pool huh ? It's cool " he joked putting his hand on his heat acting fake hurt

" what ? Neverrrr " she said kissing all over his face making him smile , he was genuinely happy with her.

" alright alright but you gotta change first " he told her while he sat on the couch looking at her while she stood infront of the tv.

" not right here imma go to your room " she started to walk to the back where she thought his room was located but was stopped as David wrapped his arms around her wait before dragging her to the couch.

" why can't you just change right here ? " he said softly in her ear sending a small chill down her spine

" uh un , I wanna change by myself sir " she replied before standing back up , fighting David's grip and gather her things to go changes

" I don't already seen everything " he shook his head looking up , licking his lips thinking of the events that happened after they went to the movies that day

" aye ! I thought I said don't bring that up again ! " she yelled from the back causing him to chuckle and make his way to the front door as he waited for her to finish

" what was the point of us coming to the pool is you wasn't gon swim ? " David asked while Chianti got on the edge of the pool and sat down , dipping her toes in.

" soo I could dip my toesss in " she smiled back at him which caused him to smirk as he got an idea.

" why you lookin at me like th- " her sentence was cut short as David kicked her into the pool causing her to submerge into the pool while David clutched his stomach as he laughed.

" oh my goddd it's could as fuck ! " she yelled as she made her way to the steps of the pool while David was still cracking up. " was it supposed to be hot ? " he teased as she gave him a death glare while going to dry off with her towel.

She sat down on the beach chair next to him staring at his figure from his tattoos to his eye that held a darkness yet loving look in them, her trance was cut short as he got a call which the caller id read 'ma dukes '.

He answered the phone and all was heard was his mother yelling about something to the extent of how he was suppose to be there to help her put up some shelf's hours ago and how she was gonna whoop his ass when he got to the house

" aight aight ma damn , I'm on my way " he looked at Chianti how nodded letting him know that she was cool with staying here by herself. He hung up the phone and they both gathered there towels and drinks before they went into the elevator, slightly shaking at the coldness from being the pool.

" aight baby I'm see you lata , my mom need me to help her with the shelf's but I won't be that long " he said as he adjusted his watch while chianti licked her lips at his appearance. Even the most simplest things he always knew how to make her feel some kinda way.

She nodded as he kissed her before leaving the apartment locking the doors and walking to the parking garage , jumping into his car before leaving.

Little did he know , somebody unexpected was watching him from a blacked out suv window , smirking as they watched David leave.

" hey ma " David nervously greeted his mother who sat on her fur chair rubbing her left thumb and pointer finger together slowly while staring at him

" uh unn don't 'hey mama' me boy , I told yo black ass to be here by 3:00 to help me and it's 5:00 boy ! You know damn well ion know how to put up no shelf's " she rolled her eyes as she lectured David.

" aight ma damn , I'm sorry ? But where these shelf's at ? " Patrice pointed to the hallway that led to the bedrooms where self parts laid neatly in the floor , as if they were waiting for him. Immediately David starting getting to work puttin them up while catching up with his mother

" soo... you still wit that lil Becky ho ? " she rolled her eyes at the thought of Emily while David laughed at his mothers description of Emily

" nah ma , I broke up with her about four , five months ago " David answered while he put the last touches on the shelf's.

A couple months into there year long fasade , Emily demanded that she met Patrice , David's mother. I didn't go very well. Patrice didn't like Emily before she had even entered the door and Emily gave her every reason to not like her.

She didn't speak when she entered the home. She tried to rush David so they could leave the whole time. She disrespect Patrice multiple times etc etc. So to hear that her son was finally done with her , made Patrice's normal mug ease up into a smile.

" soooo you talking to somebody else ? " she inquired, she already knew the answer since she heard ari giggling during there phone call.

" yea , I was with her when I was on the phone witchu , I think she tha one ma. Like no lie , she really been keepin my mind straight " David smiled as he spoke about Chianti. His mother could see the affect that Chianti had on him just by the dazed look in his eyes whenever she was brought up.

" ight we'll show me a picture of her , she betta not be white " she warned giving him a look while watching him pull out his phone from his back pocket.

He then scrolled threw his album the showcased only pictures of ari and went to find one of his favorites of her which was an off Guard , she had just finished her make up and was looking at herself in her favorite mirror , he then leaned him closer to Patrice and layed his head ok her shoulder while showing her the picture.

" this her momma " he announced as his mom looked at the picture with a smile on her face.

" oh baby she is fineee , you betta watch out and keep her close. You got yourself a beauty " his mother spoke making his heart warm that his mother liked ari at least from her picture.

" oh I already know , trust I got that on lock , but imma head back home momma , imma see you later " he kissed his mothers cheek as the exchanged goodbyes before heading back home

" bro I'm this motherfuckin close from gettin a restraining order " Chianti pinched her fingers together as she stood in front of her townhouse facing none other than domnique.

" man fuck allat , why you tellin people I'm comb ova here , that our mothafuckin business " he really just wanted a reason to come over since he hadn't in a while , he was getting a sick of emiko and he just wanted Chianti back , but he knew that she wasn't going for it.

"why the fuck are you talking to emiko you fuckin werido ?! " Chianti knew that that was the only person he could've been talkin about since that wa the only person expected David that she told.

"fosho, and been fuckin on ha , so get yo friend "he smirked feeling like he accomplished something that got under Chiantis skin , which it did but not for the reason he thought

"so you got ha pregnant is what I'm hearing ?! " she asked already knowing the answer

"obviously "he shrugged causing her to scoff and really take in what she was hearing.

"man you a bitch ass nigga foreal ! You was fuckij on my best fuckin friend or you serious?! You a bum ass bi-" domnique chocked her , pushing her up against a wall hoping to scare her into being quiet but her adrenaline wouldn't let that happen

"whatchu say ? "

"I said bum.ass.bitch."

SLAP !

Chianti hit the ground hard as her body was met with blows from left to right while Chianti covered her face to the best of her capabilities before kicking him in the balls causing him to slightly tumble over.

She crawled to the third step of the stairs to get to her house and grabbed her phone dialing 911 but as the phone started ringing she was dragged back by her foot by domnique

" imma kill yo ass I swear to god " he said before starting the beating over again "

Meanwhile at David's apartment complex he sent her a text letting her know that he was home , it was like that second his finger his the send button the doorbell rung.

" damn she here that quick " he opened up the door to see emiko standing there holding herself looking up at him.

" ummm hi." David wasn't too fond of emiko , nor did he know how she knew where he lived. To be honest he didn't really like her , he felt like something was off about her truly.

" hey , my boyfriend broke up with me " she announced looking in the background of his home while he gave a look

" how you know where I live " he questioned not really caring about her previous statement.

" I saw y'all come here after school " she answered slightly rocking back and forth on her heels.

" welp that creepy asf.. just letting you know " he shrugged and he leaned up against the doorframe debating on leaving her out here.

" I just feel like none will ever love me " she whined while David just stood there looking from side to side , getting slightly annoyed by her.

"the fuck that gotta do with me?" he asked her, she seemed shocked seeing that he was always loving and nice to Chianti so he thought it would work if she tired to do the same thing

"nooo I just need comfort from a man, you know?"

"I wouldn't know I don't like niggas" he aired, nodded a little while he silently texted Chianti about emiko being at his door

David then jumped back feeing emiko try to hug him, he lightly pushed her head back causing her to lightly stumbled back and look at him with such shock that he 'hit' her.

"ayo you gotta get the fuck like now, you highkey Harassing me and I'm not with that" he worded while emiko looked at him like she didn't understand a word he said.

"I'm crying and you won't even hug me ?! I thought I was your girl best-friend" emiko said while she shook her head at David

Thought David had called her his girl best friend once or twice, it was only beavuse Chianti told him to try to be nice to her and make her feel welcome, which he did.

"firstly, I don't even know you like that and my 'girl best friend' is my girlfriend and you most definitely ain't that." he snapped as he tried to close the door yet she pressed her whole body up against the door to stop him.

"when Chianti get here I swear I hope she whoop yo ass pregnant and all !" David warned while emiko ignored his comment still pushing in the door

" NYPD ON THE GROUND NOW ! " the nypd kicked the door down before wrestling domnique to the ground and puttin him in handcuffs.

The dispatcher ended up hearing the whole thing from the phone since Chianti never hung up and sent police to the location

" fuckkk " Chianti dragged in pain as she stood up From the ground, wiping the minor blood from off of her face and grabbing her phone seeing a text from David.

" this bitch " she murmured as she read over the text message, clenching her phone tightly in anger as her mind raced

" miss ! Are you okay ? Do you need a medic ? We can call in an ambulance " the office asked her , knocking her clear out her thoughts.

" nah , nah I'm alright , if I feel like something ain't right I'll go later , but I gotta go " she quickly said before running to her car and racing over to David's house.

" this bitch betta pray I take that baby into consideration. " she mumbled racing down the street.

" I promise I won't tell her " she tried to seduce her way into the hole but David pushed up out once again.

" ayo get the fuck out , gone now ! Do I roll yo ass down this hallway " he threatened while she pouted and folded her arms.

" I'm pregnant you dickhead " she snapped making him squint his eyes and look at her.

"and you still tranna hunch on me ? You a straight hoe I'm sorry " he laughed while she stood there straight faced.

" bro leave me the fuck alone " he said as he popped her hand as she reached out to touch him again.

Emiko seriously didn't care about Chianti or her relationship anymore c she felt like if she got one of her boyfriends she could get the other , he was just in denial is what emiko thought as she tried to reach out for him again but jumped back by the sound is a voice

" bitch if you wasn't pregnant I'd beat yo bitch ass ! " Chianti yelled as she snatched emiko back

By her hoodie causing her to stumble back off the porch.

" get her mama ! " David yelled instigated hiding behind the door slightly as she watched.

" you wouldn't let me know who to hoe ass was fuckin cause it was trey ?! Really trey of all mothafuckin people ?! Lemme ask you something cause I'm curious, if he treated me like shit the fuck made you think he would treat yo ass any fuckin different?! Huh ?! And let's talk about that fact that yo ass is 5 months pregnant and I broke up with him FOUR FUCKIN MONTHS AGO ! " Chianti yelled as emiko just stood there lightly flinching thinking that Chianti was going to hit her.

" hol up , yo what happened to yo face ?! " David flung the door opened as he got a clear glimpse of Chiantis cut and brushed face but his question was about ignored.

" which means you been sittin my my fuckin face like you my
' best friend' yet you a fuckin snake ! Asking me shit like 'how
you and trey?' Yet you fuckin him ! " Chianti lunged at emiko
but was grabbed by David who held onto her waist trying ti
calm her down

" chi calm down , she not even worth your energy " he
whispered in her ear which calmed her down slightly

" Chianti I'm sorry " emiko said , starting to cry again.

" bitch you sorry ?! " Chianti tried to lunge at her again but
was grabbed again by David.

" I'm sorry for everything , I was horrible for what I did but
I'm getting a baby out of it so you can't honestly be mad about
it " emiko shrugged trying to get Chianti to calm down.

" BITCH FUCK YOU AND THAT DAMN BA- "

" Chianti. Stop. " David said firmly causing her to not say was
she was playing in saying and saying nothing.

" you don't mean that , you'll get over it I know you will "

" nah , I meant every fuckin word. And I called police and to
dusty ass baby daddy for harassment and abuse since he don't
know how to keep his hands off of women ! " she revealed.

" wait wait wait , HE HIT YOU ?! " David shouted now his
adrenaline and anger pumping.

" I'm not even with him anymore " emiko yelled back at her

" ANYMORE ?! "

" nah nah nah , emiko get the fuck out and thus my last time , I don't hit women but I'm bout to smack yo ass " David pulled Chianti into the house while emiko finally left crying.

" I'm taking you to the hospital now and ion give a fuck watchu say , dude betta pray he don't get out cause it he do he getting handled. Period." David declared before grabbing his keys and throwing on some slides

" okay " Chianti accepted letting David carry her to the car and while they went to the hospital , their hands being held together in the middle console.

24/7

Chianti stepped out the slick shower onto the white marble floor as she slightly flinching at the cold floor. She then used her body butter that she got from the African market in new york , she let the butter substance glide across her body until her skin was smooth.

She walked out of the bathroom connected to the bedroom where David sat on the foot of the bed waiting for her with a smile on his face. " damn fat mama " he spoke as she walked up to her wrapping his hands around her and moving them down to her ass

" why yo bandaids off ? " he questioned , lightly rubbing his hands against her bruises.

When Chianti and David went to the hospital that night , the doctor did a scan on her face and bruises and just gave her a neck brace to wear for about a week. But David prescribed her to wear bandaids for a Least a couple days "come here " David guided he to the side of the bed wear she sat down and held in tightly to her robe causing him to notice and suck his teeth.

"stop acting like I ain't already seen everything "he slightly whispered kissing her neck. She smiled at him as she watched in take out the bandaids and reapply them to her face while she sat and waited patiently, she found it cute to watch him be so concentrated.

"there. All betta ma "he said as he picked her up kissing her and adjusting her in his grasp

"I gotta surprise fa you "he announced as they walked into the kitchen where designer bags stood small and large all and also a human sized stuffed bear for Chianti.

"you like ? "he asked her , slightly nervous since she hadn't said anything and was just looking at the bags and teddy bear in shock.

"I loveee ! "she dragged as she kissed all over his face , then ran to the counter talking all the bags to the bedroom and started opening them while David trailed behind her with the teddy bear in hand.

"I see you like your gifts " he said as he walked into the room to see her opening up the gifts while David snapped pictures.

"eeeeee , these are so cute I must be dreaming " she squealed as she dramatically fell into the teddy bear. He took one more picture before posting both of them in separate posts on instagram

" mannn how you look hood in everything you wear " David groaned while he watched Chianti go to his dresser wehrre her signature perfume sat, she put some Vaseline in the doors she was going to spray the perfume them applied the spray to her skin.

A

" no I don't , my face looks fucking horrible " she murmured thinking he didn't hear her , but he grabbed her waist looking at her , almost like he was searching her.

" don't ever let me hear you say some dumb shit like that again aight ? I don't date no ugly women " David said while she laughed nodding her head.

" okayyy okay , ou imma be right back I left the snacks you got me in the kitchen " she smiled and made her way to the kitchen when David phone pinged indicating a text.

" who tf ? " he mumbled to himself while oooking at the text message

" this bitch " he mumbled while making a face while he saw the text bubbles appear indicating that she was texting something else

He blocked her number as soon as he saw the bubbled reappear while Chianti walked into the room , cleaning the chocolate from around the corners of her mouth

" you full huh ? "

"nope " she smiled as she skipped towards the bed before flopping down onto the California king bed.

"gah damn , gready ass " David joked while lightly pushing Chianti who laid in her stomach , pulling down her dress.

"I'm eating fa two " she turned her head to face him , smirking as he stood up from the bed with a shocked expression.

"stop fuckin playin' you foreal ?! " he spoke excitedly while he placed both hands frimly on the edge of the bed. "nah I'm just playin witchu big dawg " she laughed slapping his chest twice.

"yo ass evil " he shook his head while he got comfortable next to her and the stuffed bear.

"so fill me in twin , what happened with emiko and shit " David questioned while he reached on his side of the bed and retrieved his rolling tray as he started rolling up.

"so she's pregnant by my ex but the thing is I broke up with him five months ago and she's now five months and a couple days , the dates match up and she told me herself so you know what that means" she explained while David made a 'yikes'

"wow , her ass weird I'm not gon lie. " He shook his head while he grinded up the weed in the grinder.

"it just hurts that I was all buddy buddy with a bitch that was real life praying on my downfall " she watched as David rolled up the grinded weed in the cigar that was emptied of its guts "when she popped up my crib talm bout' some hold me and shit , I'm like back the fuck up okay ? I value my personal space " David explained using his hands while Chianti chuckled hearing his side of the story

"and then ... sorry , she tried to take my virginity " David faked sniffled while fanning his eyes causing Chianti to suck her teeth at his dramatics

"you laughing but I was lowkey raped , she assaulted me , lucky I haven't called the police yet but I don't fuck wit 12 " David shrugged while Chianti rolled her eyes knowing he wasn't gonna let this go.

"I swear it's like she want everything I got , she lucky she got the demon semen in ha it I woulda' dragged her from here to badusala. " she promised as she slammed she left fist into her right hand.

"I'm even more pissed that she was touching up on you like girl hoe germs back it up back it up " Chianti added , fanning her hand away from her.

"barley , I was finna' push her down the steps but she said she was pregnant, kinda ruined my whole plan " David rolled his eyes and disappoint while Chianti shook her head

"and they call ME mean " she spoke to herself while continuing to shake her head while said shrugged now passing the lit blunt to her , for her to hit.

They both leaned , holding eachother like they never wanted to let go as silence took over both of them , they laid in the bed passing the blunt back and forth between eachother until it became a roach , David put the roach out then fell into sleep with his lover who he vowed to try his hardest to keep safe

" so what we gon' do ? You got anything else to blackmail him with ? "

Emiko sat poolside right next to Emily who took pictures and boomerangs of herself and emiko while they both drank cheap liquor and watched the water in the pool.

A/N : I never understood shit like this ,

like why tf you at the pool and don't get in , like take yo boring ass home ! - writer gorl

" I can find some " Emily suggested. though she seemed chill on the outside and that she wasn't bothered by David leaving her. She was breaking by the minute , realizing that the gifts , the status and other things start to go away fucked with her heavy.

So she teamed up with emiko knowing that Chianti and her had now became ex best friends and that she was east to manipulate she now had a side kick on her team which she needed.

" anything to make that bitch mad " Emily shrugged sliding in her sunglasses that covers her eyes fully.

" hood , he gone cheat on that bitch wit me , she don't even know it yet , she put domo in jail so ain't no choice but to take the other one , I don't got no job and you saw that post

he made about her earlier wit them bags , that's gone be me "
she smirked , trying to convince herself more than Emily , she
wanted Chianti's life and she wasn't going to fail on getting
it justtt yet.

"rightt her ass gon be mad .. wait she called the cops on
him , for what ?! " Emily agreed. The delusion was really a
disease.

"nothing she just was mad and watched to lie in him she
just a weird hoe " emiko explained while she rolled her eyes

"well oh well , she took my nigga do I could honestly care
less about what happens to ha'."

"he told you anything personal when y'all was together ? "
emiko questioned making Emily trace her memories of there
'relationship'.

"not really. He wouldn't tell me shit he just a closed book
though " little did she know that Chianti knew about him
within a couple months then Emily did within half a year.

"how you finna' help me then hm ? " emiko stared while
Emily sucked her teeth .

"I don't know , we'll find something though. Until then
let's just enjoy the pool " Emily suggested while they both
clunked there wine glasses together while they both laughed
to eachother.

GeTTIN' IN THE WaY

" **B** ro Emily I'm ten seconds away from hittin yo ass like you being mad desperate " David stood in the school hallway being blocked by Emily who stood in front of him trying ti get his attention as he looked above her at the exit door.

His day was going great until he went to his last class of the day which unfortunately, he had with Emily , Chianti decided to do online for a little while so her face could fully heal but David wasn't able to get online classes which sucked , but he was okay with her just having online classes.

" so your just gonna throw those months away for her ? Really ?! " Emily yelled as she stomped her foot like a five year old who hadn't gotten their way. She was still convinced that David wanted her , he was just in denial.

" yea . Correct. 100% " he responded as he pushed her out of his way heading to the exit door but she followed close behind him , hot in his heels.

" at least I won't cheat on you ! " she yelled causing David to bust out laughing , but still turn around in amusement at her accusations as stare at her.

" and what you mean by that Becky ? "

" it's Emily you dickhead , and I know she cheated on you ! You know she's pregnant right ?! " she smirked lying on Chianti , it was laughable that she truly thought David was that stupid to believe her with no proof.

" don't even try that dumb shit Emily ? Like foreal' I'll smack ya white ass bout that one and even if she was pregnant , it's because I been balls deep innat' " David laughed at the jealousy that was shown in her face

" so you like getting played huh ? Fine. You just in denial you'll be back with me soon " she smiled , still trying to follow him to his car .

" I'd kill myself before I ever got back wit yo nutty ass " he said before pushing her into a parked car and walking towards his car.

" lord , I'm not asking you to kill ha' but if you could just simply make Her disappear.... I'll go to church. " David spoke to himself as he drove into the street before turning to radio on and driving away , laughing when he sat Emily from a distance standing up from the car she was pushed into and rubbing her side heading back into the building.

" ma whea' you - damn " David leaned against the kitchen counter licking his lips while he watched Chianti pour a chit class of water from the kettle. Her hair was a different color letting him know that she must've had asmè over to do her hair , she wore a grey comfy short and shirt set. David scanned her body before finally speaking.

" David ! Did you hear anything I just said ? " she slightly pushed his head but he just laughed and shook his head no.

" I said I'm hungry as helll , I'm bout to die " she dramatically fell in the counter. David laughed as he picked her up , something that he found himself loving.

" if her come on , you not bout to starve my child " he said causing he to suck her teeth ".

" stop saying that shit , but lemme get dressed first " she rolled her eyes while she walked to his bedroom , everytime she said she was hungry or she had a attitude he would say she was pregnant.

" I'm not saying it till it becomes true ! " he announced.

" soooo "emiko awaited an updated as Emily entered the home they shared. " he would even spare a glance at them " Emily rolled her eyes , plopping down on the old couch.

" how you don't believe proof ? " emiko mumbled rolling her eyes , she wasn't used to things not going her way immediately so she was starting to get tired of chasing David. But not enough to stop doing so.

" I guess I gotta go with plan b " emiko smiled grabbing her car keys , but before she made it out the door Emily grabbed her arm and pulled her back.

" are you sure you wanna do all of this to get David ? I mean isn't this getting a little weird to you ? " truth be told , Emily wasn't even that into David anymore , she currently had her eyes in someone else. But she only continued because she felt like she was already to deep into it.

" didn't YOU blackmail him ? Now you wanna sit here and act all godly like you care ? " emiko shit back causing Emily to let her arm go and throw her hands up in defense.

" damn never mind , I was just saying I'm crazy and all... but this is a little extreme. " she admitted to herself and tried to admit to emiko who sucked her teeth , irritated by the whole conversation.

" shut up Becky " emiko rolled her eyes. " Becky ? My names Emily " Emily mumbled.

" Becky Emily same damn thing , your being really fucking unless right now " emiko put her hand on her waist getting heavily irritated by Emily.

" you know what ? Since you think you so fuckin smart. You do it your damn self. " Emily grabbing the random bottle of water in the table and splashed it in emiko's face who're leaving , slamming the door.

BLACKSKIN HEAD

The precinct smelled of depression and piss. Screams of inmates and the jingling of keys or cuffs were heard throughout the crowed place of detention. Emiko scrunched up her face in disgust looking around the walls of the jail as she walked threw the pathway with a white potbelly officer stood by her side while she walked to the back of the prison to the unfriendly looking older black lady, smacking her gum while looking emiko up and down.

"watchu need baby?" the older lady sat up straight putting her hands on the key board awaiting for further instructions by emiko.

"umm I'm bail out domnique Armani Jones" emiko smiled as the older women rolled her eyes at who happy emiko was, even though she had only met emiko not but a couple seconds ago, that smile on her face meant nothing but trouble.

" aight his bail is three thousand and your going to have to wait about an hour " the women informed her about the amount she needed for domniques bail.

" an hour ? Why can't I just give you the money and he come out , thus some bullshit. "emiko had never bailed anymore out nor had she been to a county prison before , so the process was very time consuming. Time that emiko didn't have.

The older women stopped her typing and looked at the entitled young woman who stood infront of the desk , her hand in her hip and her stank face on lock. " welcome to the county prison sweetheart " the older women gave her a sarcastic look before shooing emiko to the seat she could wait at for domnique.

An hour of scrolling threw her phone , playing in her hair and disgusting remarks about her body and face from the inmates went by before domnique came trailing out with a cop behind him , holding him by his shackles that were in his arms and legs.

" damn, you really bailed me out huh ? " domnique spoke , fake surprised. He knew that she was going to bail him out within a couple week of him being in prison, not because she needed him. But because she was stupid, she believed anything he said and all it took was one jail phone call of him claiming to love and miss her and the next day she was up here coming to his rescue.

" yup , you know I love you bae. Now we can finally start that family we was talking about " she smiled at him while he just chuckled and nodded before leaving the precinct. She dumber than I thought if she think I'm starting a family with anyone except Chianti he thought making him laugh a little louder, confusing emiko but she brushed it off.

" yo new place fye " domnique complimented casing emiko's home while she followed close behind him. She had gotten a new place shortly after domnique was out in prison for his crimes , she did it by taking some money out of domniques account. She got the account information by asking domnique in his sleep which started to get her all the answers she wanted.

" thanks , I need to baby proof everything though " she mumbled , she knew he didn't like the topic of their child because he felt like it you said that he was having a child he didn't even really care about , that meant it was true.

" mhm , how the baby doing anyway ? " he looked down at her stomach trying to seal his face from going into disgust. He wasn't happy about getting her pregnant. He was actually planning on trapping Chianti so that she couldn't leave , but it never worked.

" now you care about yo baby " emiko mumbled but domnique heard her , which is why he wrapped his right hand around her neck scaring her slightly from the unexpected attack.

" shut the shit up , i still don't even think yo ass pregnant , you might just be fat for all I know " domnique shrugged while he let her neck go.

" mmtch , I just bailed you out and you already being a dick , but anyway , we got bigger shit to focus on. Let's talk about what we gon do about Chianti " emiko smiled making Dominique sit up on the couch and give her his full undivided attention.

" all I know is I ain't going back to jail , I just got back out " domnique made that very clear to emiko , he wasn't tranna go back to jail. Jail showed him that he wasn't the top dog that he thought he was , the inmates bullied and picked on him his home time there. He wasn't going for that again.

" I got allat covered baby , trust me you ain't going back , shit gonna go just as planned " emiko smirked while she kissed domnique. She really didn't want him anymore , she wanted David. And she would do anything to get him. Yet Emily's words still ran rapid in her head , no matter how much she tried to shake them off she was really telling the truth. But emiko wasn't worried about that right now.

" bro we been in the house all dayyy " David flopped down on the bed interrupting Chianti while she was rewatching Empire. Empire and star were her favorite shows but empire was one that she rewatched religiously. And everytime she did it seemed like she missed a key part of the story. She was now on the episode when Hakeem's bride left him at the altar leaving luscious and Anika to get married.

A&N : okay but does anybody remember this episode and the DRAMA that came after jttt ?

" exactly, so I can sit in the house and catch up on empire thank you goodnight " she waved him off while she paid attention to the tv and what was happened. Now why did shine have to fuck up they weddin' like that ? She thought when she realized all of this was truly happening because of shine and him being wild before the wedding could even fully start.

" ain't luscious suppose to be dead already , I thought he had abc or rgh or sum shit " David butted in scrunching up his face when he saw what season she was on.

" firstly it's ALS stupid, and I think he ended up not having at after all , chile I don't remember just shh " she put her index finger over David's mouth signaling him to shut up causing him to suck his teeth and lay back on the headboard , crossing his arms like a child.

" so you'n wanna watch with me is watchu saying ? " she looked back at David and the face he was making at the tv. " no. Get and get dressed " he got up and pulled her by her arm off the bed causing her back to hit the ground , not hard but enough to make a slight noise.

" noooo , bro I needa find out what's gon happen next seasonnn " Chianti whined as she fought back from the grip he hand in her arm, she wasn't being too hard but he had a firm grip on her.

"mmtch , bro you don' prolly rewatched this show at least 7 times since it came out " David was absolutely right , she had rewatched it at least 7 times or more than that along with star since the shows had came out. And she wasn't ashamed to admit it.

"bro I'm surprised you don't like this show , cookie look and act JUST like your mama " Chianti stated getting up off the floor and sitting on the bed , which was true. In public she would be stopped and asking if she was the actor that played cookie Lyon , even sometimes given free stuff because of it.

"exactly, and my daddy and shit like luscious so let's go come on chi. our fridge empty and you know what happened when I left you here alone last time mama, " he softly spoke , he was scared to leave her home alone knowing about the fast of leaving her home. He kneeled down looking at her in her eyes to let her know that he was sincere and meant what he said.

"baby , domnique is in prison. he's not coming back anytime soon okay ? Me and you are safe I just wanna stay home I'm tired and I wanna catch up on my show " she stubbornly explained. It was clear that she wasn't going to budge on going to the store.

It was silent for a few seconds , David took a quick thought about leaving her home alone and though it may seem like he was being extra , he was really trying to protect her the best way he could. He sighed looked at the look she was giving which showed that she wasn't going to budge.

" Chianti. Imma lock the door , please don't open it for nobody man. " he pleaded with her, she rolled her eyes since he gave her that same speech everytime he left, even to go to the mailbox.

" okayyy , bring me some skittles " she smiled at the thought of the snack. " yea yea pregnant lady " David joked . David was dead set on them having a baby, though Chianti was more iffy on the subject, she wouldn't mind having a baby with David. She knew he would be a right dad.

" I love you mama " he whispered to her before quickly leaving , not giving her a chance to respond to what he said. He just left her there, shocked she wondered if she heard him right or maybe she mis heard his words. She figured she'd talk to him about it when he got home.

Chianti woke up from her nap to the sounds of pounding on the front door, her being tired , she forgot nearly everything David had told her before he left. She just wanted to stop the banging so she could get some sleep.

" brooo what the fuckkk " she groaned. Her feet hit the fluffy carpet as she fast walked to the front door before swinging it open she looked up but had the door forced open wider nearly hitting her in the face.

" why you call the police on me.. huh ?! " he grumbled backing Chianti into a corner who was still wiping sleep out of her eyes. " speak hoe ! " he yelled in her face not phasing her at all. After dealing with him since highschool the yelling and hitting became a regular.

" I'm not no fuckin hoe. You know why I called the police on you , you always puttin yo fuckin hands on me " reminded him which pissed him off more. Tears cascaded down her face while he laughed at her.

" stop crying fo I give yo hoe ass sum to cry about " he threatened smiling at the helplessness on her face. " " bro leaveee , I'm not playing witchu this time " Chianti spoke. " nah. You called tha police on me , you ruined me life " he explained.

" I ruined your life domnique ? I ruined your life ? That's fuckin laughable. You have NEVER had anything going for yourself , I've been there since day one DOMO and never once have you had a damn job , you life been ruined " she spoke with her hands going everywhere but everything she said went one ear and out the other.

" cap. I always had money " domnique lied. Never in his life has he had a stable income nor an come period. But Chianti didn't think of that , she mostly thought about how much she loved him. " you getting real disrespectful hoe like I won't killed yo ass right now " he said pulling out a Glock , backing her into the corner of the homes entrances.

" LEAVE NOW ! " Chianti yelling him pushing her out the door but he then grabbed her neck , hurting her putting the gun to the bottom of his neck.

"nah , I'm killing to ass right here right now " he spoke before cocking the gun back and smirking at a shaken Chianti , then the gun went off.

And domnique's body dropped.

WHO SHOT ya

S mell. Scent carries a lot of memories scientists say that if a child smells something then smells something else's nearly identical to it as an adult, they mentally go back to that place as a child.

The aroma in the room smelt of blood. Heavy breathing from Chianti was all that was heard throughout the silent apartment building , Her eyes were shut tightly and her heart feeling like it had stopped. But then she realized.. she was still alive.

She slowly opened her eyes to see that domnique was no longer standing in front of her, but laying in front of her with a hole in his chest , blood staining his white Hanes t-shirt. David stood in the walkway of the opened front door with his gun in his hand, light gun smoke coming from the barrel of the P320 M17 sig sauer.

"get up pussy" David demanded darkly , kicking the lifeless domnique in the floor, his body stayed limp on the floor. David picked up his phone and dialed a number before waiting for the other person to answer

" yooo " the person on the other end spoke , Chianti still stayed in the corner of the room her eyes wouldn't leave domnique's dead body. And oddly , she felt at peace again. Like her life was looking in the up's. Domnique was no more, and it made her smile on the inside.

" imma need you to come get this body " the person on the other end sat up and stayed silent for moment. David swore that he was out of the game because he wanted to focus on basketball. He wasn't trying to go to jail again; but apparently he decided to make an exception.

" on the way " the person hung up without needing another word as they quickly put in their shoes , grabbed their keys and left their home.

" Chianti , mama watchu crying for ? " David softly said, stepping over domnique's dead body making his way to the corner of the entrance way, she nearly fell into his arms , all he could do was hug her and let her cry.

" I- I thought I was gonna d-die David " she admitted, David sighed while rubbing her back. A feeling he knew too well.

" you don't gotta worry bout him no more ight ? His ass dead and gone " he reassured her lightly smiling when he felt her nod into his chest.

" I should've went witchu David. I swear I should've " she cried she clawed his back. The situation overwhelmed her yet gave her peace. " I know , I know. But that's neither here or there right now, I need you to pack up all your belongings I got some boxes in the closet you can use. We getting the fuck up outta this apartment " he instructed before lightly tapping her ass.

She nodded and made her way to the bedroom quickly and started packing while David roof in the entrance way looking down at domnique's body , and lightly laughing to himself emiko jayda ronad.

⌧⌧⌧ ⌧⌧⌧⌧ ⌧⌧⌧⌧ ...

It had been a week since emiko had seen or heard from domnique and it was starting to irritate her. She hadn't heard any updates about what happened with Chianti ir if he killed or injured her like the plan was.

" why tf is she texting me ? " emiko spoke aloud to herself when she saw a text come threw her phone from Emily or Becky , or whatever the girls name was.

" this shit better be worth it , cause ion got time to be getting my ass beat " emiko thought. She grabbed the keys to her Rental car and made her way out the door and to Emily's dorm that sat in campus.

" so watchu call me ova' here for ? " emiko sassily rolled her neck while standing by the door way. Her keys in one hand and her fist balled up in the other preparing for a fight.

" I'm not about to fight your weak ass emiko. I wanted to tell you that domnique is dead " the room went silent. Emiko started laughing extra loud while Emily stood there straight faced watched emiko lean over on the door and laugh.

" aye man, you not funny. Watchu' really call me over for ? " emiko smiled as her laughing settled Emily started to get angry by emiko's lack of empathy for the situation at hand. " you fuckin laughin?! You think I'm joking ? Why would I joke about what ?! " Emily screamed.

" cause you a weird bitch " emiko shrugged, the truth was the truth but you couldn't hurt someone with information they already knew.

" alright , here look ! " Emily grabbed the remote control and played a recorded news broadcasting from the day before.

" breaking news ! A young black male's body was found with a bullet wound to the chest in the east river, a couple walking around said river reported the body laying on the shore seeming to have been left there for over a week. Police have identified the man as convicted felon out on bond domnique Armani Jones known to many people as domo , family and friends devastated by the news of their loved ones passing " the women broadcaster gave out Information while a mugshot of domnique sat next to her. Emiko's mouth fell open while she watched the news broadcast speak on domnique and how he was found.

" my son would never hurt nobody man! He was a wonderful person! " her mother yelled , crying on one of domnique's homeboys shoulder " man my bro wasn't even bothering nobody! He had plans man ! He planned on getting back with his girl and building a family with ha ! Man whoever kilt my man's paying for this shit word is bond ! "his homeboy yelled into the camera before the recording ended.

"man who kilt him ?! " emiko yelled questioning Emily who held her hands up in defense. " I don't know nobody does , but you said he went over their to kill chianti right ? Shit that seems like his karma " Emily slightly laughed shrugging , getting up from the couch and going to the kitchen pouring herself something to drink.

"man I don't believe in that shit ! It's clear he was killed ! " emiko scream cried.

" did you tell ? "she questioned , powering walking towards Emily who stood across her kitchen island drinking her juice.

" what ? Girl no why would I call you over here just to have snitched in you ? Like you make no since "Emily sarcastically asked her leaving emiko to sit there and think.

" okay so how you the first one to know he died ?! " she screamed. " emiko are you fuckin dumb ? everybody knows ! How the fuck do you not know ? Why aren't YOU keeping tabs on YOUR baby daddy ? Huh ? That shit was on the news , his homeboys posting him on social media. You to busy being a dick chaser you can get the fuck out." she she snapped before grabbing her cup full of juice and leaving the room leaving emiko sitting there. Tears cascading down her face.

" this some bullshit. " was the last thing emiko muttered in Emily's kitchen before yanking the front door open and slamming it shut. She was determined to find out what happened to domnique.

chianti nian london.

" fuck ! " David groaned before slamming into Chianti's wet honeypot on last time before nutting in her , Chianti lost her arch as she laid flat on the bed , her eyes closed as she slowly came down from her high.

" girl , if yo ass wasn't pregnant before , you definitely is now " David laughed as he slapped her ass while she turned her head to look at him.

" why you talking bout getting me pregnant so muchhh " she laughed while she laid on top of David , getting under covers in the warmth , her hand drawing circles on his chest.

" cause I want a lil me or lil you. And only with you " David confessed kissing her cheek. David was always a baby lover , he had always dreamt of having a family with a woman he loved and being the father that he never got to have. And Chianti was everything he wanted in a wife, there was no if ands or buts, Chianti was going to be his wife and the mother of his kids. Point blank.

" I lowkey ain't' really crazy for kids " Chianti shrugged causing David to sit on in bed , with Chianti still in his arms. " why ? " he questioned , most of every woman he met wanted to have his kids , so to see one who wasn't crazy about the idea, intrigued him.

"they to much to handle , plus I don't have much experience dealing with them " she answered while David listened intensively. "that's why they got to parents duh" he shrugged kissing her on the forehead before pressing in it causing her to laugh.

"ight so what if we break up , then I'm jest the babymomma " she remarked throwing her hands in the air. "nah that ain't gone happen " he insisted shaking his head.

"and how you know that ? " she inquired looking at him with her eyebrow raised in a questionable matter.

"stop worrying Fathead , you don stress our child out " he muttered the last part but Chianti still heard her , hints why she sucked her teeth.

"shut yo ass up " she rolled her eyes lightly pushing his arms causing him to laugh and change his position to where he was laying ontop of her holding himself up , his chain dangling in her face.

"make me." he whispers in her ear while she lightly gasped from the quick change in the position they were in. She the. Took control in the situation and flipped them over getting on top of him. Them both being naked.

"bet."

new Beginnings

X ☒☒☒☒☒ ☒☒☒☒☒..

"imma make sure nothing happens to that pretty face again" David softly kissed all of the spots Chianti's healed bruises used to be at while she sat on their master bathroom sink in their new home.

That's right, David and chianti both moved into a new home together a month back. Both names where on the lease but David refused to let her pay a bill. They did have a slight argument but they came to in agreement that if he payed all the bills, she would pay for all the new furniture and appliances. The home's color scheme ranged from dark grey, black and royal blue which David loved, they both liked the dark yet light color scheme.

"I know you will" she reassured him before jumping off the counter and walking into the bedroom, he watched as her ass swayed while she walked to the bathroom. David's phone rung on the top of the toilet and the caller id read " herbo " so he laughed slightly and answered

" yooo " he answered the phone , walking to the bedroom where Chianti came to view. She scrunched up her eyebrows when she saw his phone to his ear wondering who he was on the phone with.

" what is that " she mouthed causing him to mouth back "herb" making Chianti roll her eyes and went back to scrolling on her phone. Chianti made it known that she didn't fuck with herb though she never met him, the stories she heard about him from David caused her to already feel some type of way about him and his play boy antics.

She knew he had a girlfriend , she didn't know what she looked like in person but she saw pictures of her and she was beautiful. The first thing she thought when she saw a picture of her was 'how the fuck did herb bag that?' But nonetheless. She next it alone

" yoo was good man , we ain't' chilled in awhile so I was thinkin since you with chi I was thinking we could do like a lil double date hang out " herb suggested. David looked at Chianti to get her opinion on the suggestion to see her emphatically shaking her head no causing David to laugh and smirk

" yea we'a be there lata " he let herb know looking at Chianti who sucked her teeth and stomped off to the kitchen. " ight bet , see you in a few one." Herb hung up. He shook his head before walking ti the kitchen where Chianti stood there talking shit ti herself pouring a glass of wine.

"why you mad girl ? I get you'n fuck wit herb like that but his girl new new gon be there " he hummed knowing that she would decide to come if new new was their since she'd been wanting to meet her in person for ever. However she sighed and finally spoke "okay " she finally accepted laughed at David's 'yes' dance.

"yes yes yes , aight be ready a couple minutes cause we bout to leave " he announced before going back to the bedroom to put in some clothes himself.

chianti nian london.

Chianti sat in the passenger seat on instagram posting a picture of her and David she took earlier at the house when they pulled up to herb house , she looked up at the home and sighed slightly annoyed that she even agreed to come and David noticed.

He put the car in park and stared at her to which she ignored his gaze before he took his fingers and moved her face to match his gaze. " be nice aight' ? we only gon be in hea for a lil while I'm just bout to chop it up for a minute " he told her to which she just nodded her head and let him get out the car , then come around to her side and open up her door holding out his hand and helping her out the car.

"yooo wassap boy ! I ain't seen you in a brick minute ! " herb enthusiastically stood up from the couch and dabbed his home boy up while David laughed and greeted him the same way.

"wassap nigga good to see you ! But this my wife Chianti , Chianti this is Lauren " David introduced her to Lauren , herbs girlfriend who sat on the red couch.

a women stood up from the couch with a small and warm aura on her face , her deep dimples showed nicely on her face. Her pictures definitely didn't do justice to the beauty that she truly was and Chianti definitely wanted to be her friend.

"heyy boo I'm Lauren nice to meet you girl , your pretty has hell by the way " she complimented sticking her hand out for a handshake but Chianti quickly pulled her into a tight hug that she didn't know was much needed.

"thank you girl , your beautiful as hell too , but I'm lowkey hungry " Chianti stated while Lauren pulled away from the hug and stepped back. " ouu I made a seafood boil for us , imma go get it , yall sit down and get ready " Lauren smiled before walking away.

"so how long y'all been together ? " Lauren quizzed while she sucked the extra meat from out of the carb leg she held in her hand.

"about 5 - 6 months I believe , how about yall ? " Chianti answered laying her head on David's shoulder while he tour the sea food boil a new one.

" 2 and a half yea- we been on and off but yeah 2 and a half years " herb disrespectfully cut Lauren off making sure that they new they were on and off , we'll more like chainti knew that they were off and on." aww okay " chainti mumbled getting annoyed by him interrupt their conversation

" soo , no babies yet ? " David chuckled nervously trying to change the obvious shift in the emotion in the room.

" no , he don't want none " Lauren rolled her eyes looking at herb. " Lauren don't start that shit " he tired to silently grit towards her but she said nothing , just hummed a small response.

" all I said was you don't want none , calm down "she rolled her neck at his random attitude." yea whatever "he responded and kept eating the seafood.

" it's the other way around , chi don't want none at all " David announced while chainti kept eating her foods " correct " she commented.

" why not girl ? " Lauren asked , not many girls she met didn't want kids but it was clear that Chianti was very serious about not wanting kids

" they too much for me , especially for my career choice I'm going for " chainti answered shrugging.

" but you'll have David for help , cause by the way his hand wrapped around you it's clear you ain't goin' nowhere " Lauren joked at the fact that David had his arm wrapped tightly around Chiantis neck.

" that's exactly what I said , but she got a small brain so I be having to talk slow sometimes " David shrugged causing chainti to lightly slap him across the head.

" You just wanna get getcho' ass whooped I f torn if your lil friend " chainti insisted while Lauren laughed. Meanwhile herb sat in the corner all mopy and kept giving chainti weird puppy eyes

" we bout to dip though , cause I can tell chi getting full and tired " chainti was slumped over in her chair with her head laying on the top of the chairs head rest with her eyes closed but she was still awake.

" aight boo umm see you lata but gimmie your number " Lauren suggested while herb smirked at the two conversating while they exchanged numbers.

" ight cool imma see you lata boo " chainti kissed Lauren's cheek as they left out the house. Herb stood up from his seat locking the door behind them while Lauren stayed in the kitchen cleaning the table and throwing away the trash from the seafood boil.

Herb walked into the kitchen watching Lauren intently while she cleaned with her back turned towards him however , she felt him staring and stopped cleaning before turning around and looking at him.

" what I told you bout' that baby shit ? Why the fuck you keep mentioning that shit man ? " herb interrogated her cause if her to suck her teeth. They had this argument every other day whenever she mentioned anything slightly dealing with babies.

"bro you really starting this shit today ? All I said was that you don't want one and your still on that shit ? " Lauren sighed , that was something that she hated about herb. He would dwell on arguments all day then finally decided that he wanted ti talk about it when everything was cool and chill.

"you didn't have to say allat shit ' you not finna' try and make me feel bad for not wanting a fuckin baby withchu ' ! " he yelled whine she just stared at him like he was crazy them lightly scoffed and chucked , gathering her things that were in the kitchen with her.

"aight cool , if that's your word then cool , not even finna go back and forth with you" she quietly spoke before speed walking to there bedroom. Herb shrugged not following after her before going to the living room and turning on the tv.

Meanwhile with David and Chianti they were both chilling at their new house when a knock came from the door. They both looked at eachother in confusion since they didn't invite anyone over but they still went to the door and looked through the people hole , sucking there teeth at who was at the door

"what you want ? " chainti snapped , shifting her leg weight from one to the other seeing emiko standing at the door

"chi , domnique died " she said expecting a reaction out of Chianti to which she got none. " okay ? Was I supposed to cry

? " chainti quizzed while laughing with David while emiko sat there in the doorway looking stupid.

" how ? That's your ex Chianti ! " she yelled slightly tearing up by her non caring reaction to the news of emiko's baby father's death.

" mhm. Why you here again ? "

" listen , I know we fell off bad but I miss our friendship. I miss when we used to comfort eachother - key word used to " chainti cut her sob story off to which emiko ignored .

" I know what I did was fucked up but I'm sorry chi , please forgive me " emiko was extremely lonely now that Emily am had seen the error of her ways , now it was just her and her now unwanted child. She needed support , and she wanted it from chainti.

" you can leave now " chainti ignored her apology causing emiko's face to change from sad to angry.

" wow , so your just going to throw years of friendship away ? Really ?! " emiko yelled " yep and don't care , now get the fuck out for I whoop yo ass " chainti threatened when David walked into the mix

" what goin on mama ? " he questioned but when emiko saw him , she smiled. " heyy David " she dragged greeting him but he just gave her a weird look.

" ew " he said before backing out of the room and going back into the living room.

" wow y'all made fake i swear " emiko adjusted her fake Gucci bag on her arm making chainti laugh at her statement of them being fake.

" I'm fake but you was fuckin off my boyfriend? " chainti asked while emiko just stood there " ex. " she mummered correcting chainti

" you was fuckin him when he was together Ian dumb Jayda " chainti called her by her middle name rolling her eyes.

" no we wasn't Chianti " emiko lied, on the inside she was shaking that chainti knew that they were fucking when they were together , she was thanking God that she was pregnant cause she knew if she wasn't , her ass would've been busted up by now.

" sure emiko , you just be lying like it's nothing huh ? Ion even know why im still talking to you , get the fuck outta hea " she demanded , opening the front door and moving to the side for emiko to leave

" please can I just vent ? I don't have nobody to all to " she cried trying to gain a little bit of sympathy from chainti which she got none.

" me and David fucked ! " emiko yelled causing David to run to the entrance to see why the fuck his name was being mentioned. " no the fuck I didn't weirdo ! Get the fuck out like foreal ! " David pushed her out of the walkway watching her stumble back

" this why I can't fuck witchu no more , case you always fuckin lyin , now for the last time. Get the fuck of my porch for I forget you pregnant " chainti threatened making emiko run towards her car in fear.

" and don't come back either ! " David yelled slamming the door and walking to the living room where Chianti was laying ont the couch. " bitches be bonkers " she mumbled causing David to laugh.

Just then , a random number texted chainti's Phone , so David being David he checked the message.

David scrunched his face seeing that the number looked really familiar to him , so he pulled out his phone and went to his recents just to realize

It was herbs number.

redemption

P EOPLE talking among themselves in the crowded restaurant while chianti's leg rapidly shook while she waited for Lauren. It had been a week since the incident of herb trying to get wit chianti and needless to say , chianti and David decided to confront the two about the messages.

While David was on his way to herb and Lauren's residence, chianti sat at a restaurant in a booth in the far right corner waiting for Lauren to walk threw the front door with the text message thread printed out in her hands. Her palms started to profusely sweat when she saw Lauren enter the restaurant and start to visibly search for Chianti until her eyes landed on her , lifting up her hand and signaling her to come over.

Lauren held her Chanel bag on her shoulder as she walked towards the table hugging Chianti before sitting down smiling, her dimples being visible.

"hey boo ! Girl sorry we couldn't meet up earlier, I been so busy with herb and ugh just everything" Lauren rolled her eyes jokingly. Chianti's stomach turned at the mention of the unloyal basterd known as herb

" oh…. Okay. Well girl I just wanted to show you something …" Chianti nervously spoke before sliding the stack of papers towards Lauren and allowing her to read them.

Lauren read threw the sexually explicit messages showing herb asking chainti for different sexually favors and even telling her that he would leave Lauren if she gave him a chance. He brought up a lot about there relationship and most importantly: about Lauren's miscarriage.

When lauren and herb where in their first year of dating lauren got pregnant , but four months into her pregnancy she was jumped by who she know knows as herbs ex Latiana and her friends resulting in her miscarriage. After that it was like herb wasn't in live with her the way he used to be.

He wasn't loving , caring etc. he was basically just there, and that wasn't something that Lauren felt comfortable with. but knowing how his explosive behavior was , she decided to just deal with it and pray that things finally went back to the way they were.

But this. This was conformation. He didn't live her anymore , nor was he interested in being in a relationship with her anymore. Her hand slowly started to shake in angrier as tears rolled down her face before she set the papers down.

" listen Lauren , boog , niggas like these are not worth your tears. And his ass is ugly as fuck anyway so it's not really like you missin' anything " Lauren slightly laughed nodding her head and wiping her tears taking his what Chianti was telling her.

" girl real shit , thank you for telling me about this. Like you truly a real bitch. Cause most females would've just kept it to themselves and let their friends walk around lookin' stupid… but you didn't. Thank you girl " Lauren stood up from the table and reached out for a hug from Chianti which she gladly expected.

" girl no problem, you my friend. I'm not just going n let you walk around looking dumb. That's jus not cool. but aye make sure you treat his ass accordingly " chainti lectured causing Lauren to wave her hand.

" nah I already got that under control, matter fact I gotta go I need to go get some things " Lauren grabbed her things silently smirking to herself at the mischief she was planning on causing in her home.

" ight girl , call me later I wanna know what happened " chainti sipped her glass of half and half making Lauren laugh and nod. She didn't wanna seem messy , but she still wanted to know how shit went down.

" aight peace out " Lauren threw up the peace sign. They both exchanged goodbyes and Lauren left leaving Chianti alone in the booth. After a couple minutes she finally called the police sitter over to ask for the check and a box for her meal as she sat back wondering how David and her a conversation was going.

david mani brewster.

DAVID sat on herbs couch as if he hadn't just let himself in by picking the locks. Herb was preoccupied on the bathroom toilet while FaceTiming latiana , feeding her the same lies he did everytime they FaceTimed.

David scrunched his nose up at the stench and hay came from the hallway bathroom herb was in. He shook his head getting bored waiting for him to come out of the bathroom since he had been sitting in the living room for a good twenty minutes so he decided to check Chianti's story to see what she was up too.

David smiled at the picture Chianti posted of them when they were walking the streets of New York, talking and smoking a blunt after there picnic was semi ruined by the unexpected cold weather.

David put his phone away when he heard the bathroom door open and herb's footsteps walking towards the kitchen. He had always wanted to sneak up on somebody so this was nothing but pure fun for him.

" expecting someone ? " herb squealed at the unexpected voice of David sitting in his couch hunched over with his elbows sitting on his knees, his hands being held together. It was clear herb was expecting a female that definitely wasn't Lauren since he held a wine bottle and condoms in his hand knowing that Lauren was on birth control so it was clear he was expecting latiana.

" man watchu' doin here in tha fuckin' dark ! " herb clenched onto his chest laying lightly on the wall to catch his breath by the unexpected scare.

" yea nigga fuck allat'. Come sit ... let's talk. " David patted the seat the farthest to the right next to him. Herb nervously nodded before slowly sitting down on the couch. He knew what he had did , he just didn't know is David knew what he had did.

" you know I'm always with her right ? " David questioned after a moment of slime fell between the two.

" Ian een' text her " herb blurted out to try and save his ass. but the only thing he did was seal his fate.

" I didn't say shut about you texting' her " david slowly stood up and stood in front of herb , towering over him since herb was sitting and David was now standing.

" whatchu talm' bout " herb scrunched up his face trying to play dumb and act like he didn't saw what he just said.

" ayo don't test my gansta' , cause word up I'll kill your right here , right now. " David threatened pushing his gun that sat in his hoodie pocket to the show the print of it.

" aight ! Aight ! Chillat! All this shit over a bitch ?! " herb yelled holding his hands up In defense. David grabbed his by the neck line of his shirt catching herb by surprise. " say some shit like that bout my lady again and Imma really kill yo ass " he whispered being that he was close to herbs face, but not too close ... cause that's gay.

"aight bro chill ! " he screamed after David let him go. " like I said , you not my fuckin' bro no more " David shook his head , backing away from her.

" all this over a female mane ?! " herb asked correctly, him personally he would never drop his homie for Lauren. If it came down to either or , his homie would be the one he'd pick. You know..... CAUSE HE'S A BITCH.

" over MY female , my woman , my fuckin' wife damn near like you really gon try and sit here and try to text and fuck on mines ? Yo you know fa a fact that was some snake ass shit " David paced the floor while he spoke.

" I didn't know y'all was that serious " herb mummered looking down at the ground , as if he was a child in trouble that the principals office.

" I don't matta' if we was or not ! nigga at this point you asking for me to kill ya bitch ass " David pulled out the gun and cocked it causing David to lightly grab the gun. " david chill tha fuck out ! ".

" nah nigga cause lemme tell you sumthin' ion play bout' mines " david tapped his chest lightly. " ight , ight my bad " herb held his hands up In front of his face afraid from his life.

" that's all you gotta say ? " david titled his head smirking at how herb begged for mercy. Herb shrugged causing David to shake his head and laugh slightly before leaving out of the home , slamming the door behind him. leaving herb to finally exhale a breath he didn't even know he was holding.

aftermath

T HE car stereo clock striked three o'clock am as Lauren pulled into the long driveway of the home her and herb once shared. Her finger nail tapped lightly up against the steering wheel as she got her thoughts together before getting out the car and grabbing the baby oil she purchased earlier that day.

She quietly used her key to enter the home before tiptoeing up the stairs and entering the bedroom where herb laid comfy under the covers that were bought by Lauren. She shook her head but continued to make her way to the closet and get all of her belongings, not caring if her woke up or not.

" hell you doin ? " herb rasped out sitting up in bed while his eyes adjusted to the darkness of the room. Still ignoring herb , Lauren grabbed more of her belongings and put them in one of the many trash bags she had brought with her.

" getting me stuff " she mummered out but herb still heard her " for ? " he asked as if he hadn't slept with latiana not but a couple hours ago.

" don't worry bout' it " Lauren seethed, her back still turned towards him, she started to pile her heels and sneakers into a big trash bag. Herb roughly got up from the bed dressed in nothing but a wife beater and some boxers and stared angrily at the back or Lauren's head.

" the fuck you mean don't worry bout' it ?! Lauren don't fuckin play wit me , I'm tired man. " herb was not only a very angry person in general , but he was also a little hung over causing his anger levels to triple there normal levels.

" ain't nobody playin witchu , I said what the fuck I said ! If you don't know immediately why I'm acting like this , figure it out Herbert " Lauren scoffed folding a shirt and putting it in the trash bag , then sitting the trash back onto the bed causing them to now be face to face.

" bro Lauren - " he started taking a deep breath and running his hand down his face before shaking it " can you just communicate wit me ma ? Like we ain't kids nomo' what the fuck is wrong with you " herb tried to sound sincere trying to play the victim once again.

Lauren stopped her movements and looked up at herb for a second before laughing confusing herb " ya'know ... it's so fuckin' amazing to me how you can sit up here and act like you ain't did shit ".

"what I do ? "herb scratched the top of his head , a common thing he did when he was lying or about to make up a lie.

"Why when you know " she spoke before she started throwing stuff into her trash bag , trying to get out of the place she once called home as soon as possible.

" if this is about then text wit Chianti - " Lauren scoffed again before cutting him off " see! Exactly, you just proved my damn point. Lying like you ain't do shit " Lauren rolled her eyes before picking up another garbage back and starting to fill that one up.

"man , Lauren I didn't - "lauren threw her hand up in his face causing him to silence his speaking. " don't wanna hear it , goodnight and goodbye " she stated before walking slightly off of the room and setting the garbage bag in the side of the door frame.

" bro why won't you just trust me ? " he sat on the side of the bed trying to seem as innocent as humanly possible.

" trust you ? Haven't we gon threw this cheatin' shit before ? And you think your worthy of my trust ? Tuh ' " she laughed going back to the closet and starting on her coats , sunglasses and winter clothes.

" man please ! It's just sumthin' I gotta do first before I tell you bae " he walked to the closet and tried to wrap his arms around her waist to which she grabbed the baby oil in her pocket and squirted it in his face causing his to stumble back.

She then grabbed the nearest belt which was her Chanel rhinestone belt and started to slap in viciously with it , her tried to grab onto the belt but slipped and what now laid on the carpet while Lauren continued her assault.

Once she was finally well and ready. She continued to collect her clothes while herb laid in the closet floor in pain crying. She finally left, making her to lock up his home deciding to give the house key to a very nice homeless man that hung around there neighborhood.

" twenty twenty vision, city girls winnin' coping is both shit " chainti looked at david to finish the statement.

" Chianti , you been singing that shit for 4 fuckin' hours. No I'm not sayin it again " david kept his eyes on the tv while he felt Chianti staring a whole j to the side of his head.

" bruh " david sucked his teeth seeing that Chianti was still blankly staring at him causing him to take a deep breath " bitch we twininnnn " he finally said making chainti smile and laugh.

It was clear that he was becoming very soft for her , any-thing she wanted form him she got it and as you've seen , he wasn't afraid to kill for her.

" you hungry ? " he shifted his head to look at her while she laid next to him in her phone.

" duhh pookieee " she dragged , pookie had became a new favorite nickname for him , at first he hated. But know he'd grown used to it , and slightly took a liking to the name.

"ight bald head let's go " David joked standing up front the bed causing Chianti to suck her teeth , he'd been calling her 'bald head' every since he walked in on her installing a wig with her wig cap on.

"boy you just mad because I got more hair than you , don't play " she rolled her eyes and David did the same , copying her.

"I thought I told you to break them up "emiko started to get very bratty , and was irritated that Chianti and David where still together. You would think after losing nearly everything she owned she would stop trying to break them up, however , it was the only thing that kept her going .

She had lost Emily , who she was now realizing was a pretty good friends to her , only with her bestfriend chianti, then she lost her child's father domnique. And because he died leaving nothing behind for her or their child, his mother and homies inherited the house emiko bought , and everything in it , including some of her clothes.

"man I tried. And I can't keep doin' this shit , it's ruining my relationship " herb complained laying on the cotton mat emiko called her bed. Herb was still in denial that Lauren was actually done with him. To him , she just needed her space and she'd come crawling back.

However , that was very for from the truth. Lauren was already looking for apartments far away from herbs home , even thought David and Chianti offered for her to stay with them , she decided to give the couple their privacy and get a hotel.

"come be with me then , I'll treat you better " at this point , emiko was desperate for someone. Someone with financial stability to be exact. And herb was the best best candidate other than David.

"yeaa nah. Ion want no crazy bitch like you. I want my new new back " herb declared. It was like his life went downhill every since he decided to go along with emiko's plan.

"true " emiko shrugged.

"man I'm not bout' to keep doin this shit , you obsessed with that girl man " herb exposed.

"so you don't wanna do it no more ?! " emiko yelled , her mood going from smooth and calm to irate and uneasy. She stood up from the mat and stood over herb who looked up at her with a blank face.

"no. I already got my girl thinkin' I purposely cheated wit' you "yes herb didn't only text Chianti , but he slept with emiko a couple days after that. A true dog nigga.

" don't act like you didn't like it " emiko said seductively biting her lip.

"I didn't. Like at all. And now she think I'm cheatinn' again " herb rolled his eyes and put his head down , frustrated at himself for allowing himself to be In such predicament.

"oh well , you might as well be with me " emiko tried to persuade with a smile.

"bro , YOUR THE REASON SHE THINK IM CHEATIN'! YOU DEADASS TEXTED CHIANTI FROM MY PHONE ! AND TRYIN' NOT TO GETCHO DUMBASS MOLLY WHOOPED , I SAID IT WAS ME ! "

"cause you know what the fuck would've happen if you said anything. And she already think you cheatin' might as well do it anyway " she shrugged , emiko was unfazed by the hole situation, she had already ruined her and her unborn child's life , she had nothing and no one else to lose but she wasn't stopping until chianti and david were not together anymore.

"nah. I'm done wit this shit " herb shook his head getting up off the mat and standing by the entrance of her run down apartment.

"you know what happens is you back out right ? " emiko wasn't about that life at all. But she'd use herself to get what she wanted , and she had no level of low she wouldn't stoop that low to.

"you sick as fuck , obsessed with a nigga that don't even like you like that " herb laughed causing emiko to shrug.

"so what I want him , and I will ruin your life if you don't help " she folded her arms like a toddler would smirking.

"ion got shit fa you too ruin , you don already did that shit , so shut the fuck yo and get a damn life " he stated unlocking her home door and walking out

"JUST WAIT ! " she opened the door sticking her head out watching him walk towards his car causing him to throw her the bird and continue walking.

can't get in my feelings

"Damn girl , who blowing you up ? " Chianti laughed making Lauren roll her eyes. Lauren and Chianti had became very close since the whole herb thing , actually they had became close to bestfriends very quickly.

" girl it ain't nobody but herb , nigga keep textin' me off of random numbers " Lauren explained blocking the third number that had texted her.

" girl fa what " Chianti scrunched up her face in disgust. Just by what Lauren had told them about their relationship in a whole , she was nothing short of disgusted with herb.

" he said he just wanted to talk , but I'm not really with even seeing him at all " Lauren confessed shrugging her shoulders before setting her phone face down on the couch.

" like a week ago when I went over there to get my stuff he wash like oh it's some stuff he can't tell me but he'd tell me today " Lauren explained , Chianti came out the kitchen with her favorite bottle of red wine sitting it on the coffee table before sitting next to Lauren.

"that's a lil weird" Chianti said pouring herself a glass. "you know ion even like her.. like at all, but maybe you should see what he gotta say" Chianti gave her advice shrugging before taking a sip of her wine. "you don't gotta take him back, but you should just see what he gotta say" chainti ended leaving lauren in thought as she pouted her own glass of wine.

"you right, I will lata' but right nowwww I'm tryna get tipsy" Lauren stuck her tounge out pouring her a large portion of wine.

"I know that's right" Chianti agreed.

"alright alright, s'cuse me" David pushed Lauren out the way sitting in between the two women laying his head on Chiantis breast.

"so I hen can I get my girl back miss new new" David asked seeing that the girls had been in the living room drinking glass after glass for a good two hours.

"David shush" chainti popped him the the face causing him to suck his teeth.

"nah patchy's fine, I need to be heading out anyway" Lauren laughed standing up feeling fine. Lauren could hold her alcohol very well so the wine she had really didn't hit her much. She was buzzed at the highest but she was overall fine to drive.

" baby , you not gon defend me ? She brought up my patches baby.... My patches " David faked cried caressing the patches in his beard

" David you betta calm down , acting like a damn child , but I'll call you lata Lauren so we con continue our conversation alone " Chianti told Lauren who was standing by the door

" I don't know why you say that like y'all was really spillin' some real tea , yall girl talk was boring as hell , " David spoke causing Chianti to suck her teeth

" then why was you in here ear hustling " Chianti asked playing in his hair. His braids were out because today was wash day and Chianti was suppose to braid his hair once Lauren left.

" cause I wanted to stare at cho pretty ass that's why " David mumbled kissing her cheek and going back to laying on her chest getting in aww from Lauren.

" mmtch , imma leave y'all two love birds to it , BYE ! " Lauren said before laughing and jokingly slamming the door on her way out of the home leaving the two alone in the couch while the get up on Netflix played.

" FINALLY ! i get my baby back " David dramatically threw his head back picking chianti up and taking her into their bedroom.

" aww pookie " she teased knowing that he hated that name , she first started calling him that as a joke but it became a name she enjoyed calling him.

" you really like that nick name ? " david genuinely asked tilting his head causing Chianti to nod smiling

" you lucky I love you enough to let you call me that " David shook his head flopping onto the bed and laying on his side facing her.

Chainti started to speak about her day and random things she was interested in at the moment and like always David listened , however half way threw her rant David zoned out staring at her. His heart warmed as he watched her smile talking about the things that interested her , and his heart went even warmer when he imagined coming home to her and their future child.

" I wanna get you pregnant , we'll talk about to wigs lata " david spoke lightly tossing Chianti's phone to the side of the bed before getting on top of her sharing a passionate kiss.

" you know you not gettin' me pregnant today right ? " chainti stopped him before he took off her panties

" of course , we practicin' " he winked causing her to smile and giggle as he kissed her sweet spot on her neck.

" alright whatchu' call me here fa " Lauren sat down her dior tote bag on the arm of the couch of the place she used to call home. Herb sat in front of her his head placed in his hands before he looked up at her.

His heart dropped even more when he realized how good she looked without him. Her skin glowed , she had put on some more happy weight just within the couple weeks they hadn't been together while herb on the other hand was breaking more by the hours.His eyes were covered with bags , it looked like he hadn't ate in weeks and thought Lauren felt sorry for him , she had already made up her mind. Him and her would never be a thing again.

" you gon talk or you just gon keep staring at me " Lauren knocked him out of his trance tilting her head to the side

" my bad. You look good " her nervously chuckled getting no response from her.

" aight , I'm sorry for treating you the way I did durning our relationship. I never showed you affection, and I'm sorry for that." he began "you prolly think ion give a fuck bout you' but I do. Foreal shawty " herb ended.

" alright. Is that All you brought me here to say " Lauren asked standing up from the couch picking up her purse getting ready to leave.

" wait hol' up " herb grabbed onto her arm Turning her to face him." I wasn't the one that texted her man , but I couldn't tell you who did " herb tried to explain but Lauren wasn't trying to here any of it.

" still don't get how you couldn't tell , like the fuck does that mean " Lauren's neck moved wildly as she spoke

" emiko texted her. She grabbed me my phone " herb blurted out ringing silence into the home.

" how did she have your phone ? " Lauren asked causing herb to stay silent. Lauren chuckled at the look on his face knowing the answer

She shook her head before picking up her back and leaving.

real love

" I gotta pee " Chianti randomly spoke out. Her and david drive down the streets of newyork in David's new car , as usually david hadn't let her know what they were doing nor where they were going. He just simply told her to get up and get dressed in a comfortable outfit.

" ight pissy " David mumbled turning into a near by gas station , " shut up " Chianti smacked his chest playfully as he laughed , parking the car for her to get out and go into the bathroom.

" this shit is nasty " Chianti mumbled to herself as she entered the rundown gas station bathroom , hovering over the seat.

David and Chianti entered the bowling alley going straight towards the ticket booth where a young woman , seeming to be a couple years older then the two , stood.

" aye , lemme get two tickets and two pair of bowling shoes , men size 11 and female size 7 please " David said casual voice. The woman finally looked up before biting her lip at the tall man in front of her , not even realizing his girlfriend was right next to him, nor caring either.

" aight " she responded , going to the back and coming back out a couple moments later with two tickets and the shoes. " here you go " she smiled seductively, caressing his hand when she handed him the ticket.

" ew " David damn near yelled. jumping his hand back ,getting the attention of Chianti who stood behind him on her phone.

" what ? " the woman asked with sass in her tone , popping the imaginary gum she was chewing.

" yo lash falling off " he pointed out as if he was a child. " don't worry my girl might have some lash glue " he told the woman before turning to Chianti who was holding back laughter.

" my lash is not falling off " the woman sassed again , rolling her eyes. David leaned over to

Look more closely before he scrunched up his face in dis-gust

" you right , yo shit's not even on yo damn lash line , dem hoes is damn near on yo eyebrow. Ew " David shook his head as if he was disappointed before he snatched the shoes and tickets and started marching towards their lane.

" you wrong as hell fa that " Chianti let him know while she laughed walking In front of him.

" aye , it ain't my fault I was tryna help her loose lash having ass out " David threw his hands up in defense causing chainti to just shake her head and sit in the seats on their lane , putting in her shoe's while David did the same.

" ayeee I won , I wonnnn , I really really wonnn " Chianti chanted while he and David walked out of the bowling alley , hand in hand.

" yo happy ass " David mumbled , slightly pouting. " don't be mad cause yo ass lost " Chianti joked laughing her way towards the car.

" yea yea whatever , I know yo lil ass hungry , where you wanna eat at ? " David asked while he opened up her car door , letting her get settle in before he slammed the door shut , then jogged over to his side of the car and got in also.

" ion really care , I'm just hungry " Chianti shrugged causing David to nod and start the car allowing Chianti to pick the song which was stand out off of the goofy movie soundtrack. David had came to realize that Chianti was very deep into Disney music , she even showed him some hidden bangers , one of his favorite's she had showed him was ev'rvbody wants to be a cat and thomas O'Malley cat from the aristocats soundtrack.

Life Goes on

☒ ☒☒☒☒☒ ☒☒☒☒☒.

"David this is my third time callin' you , I swea' I can't take my eyes off of you for more that five minutes! I swear you like a damn five year old. Once I find ya ass .. ouuu you ain't seein' daylight for a while nigga ! " Chianti yelled into her phone , tapping her foot against the hardwood floors in Zara , a popular clothing store in the mall.

"I'm right here mom " David sarcastically responded standing right behind Chianti the whole time and recorded her lengthy voicemail.

"oh .. well then ignore allat " she instructed smiling up at him. David shook his head , "you ass been acting' crazy as hell lately " he voiced jokingly.

Chainti's face fell at the statement and before she knew it , tears started to stream down her cheeks leaving David in a state of confusion.

life had been good for chainti and david. emiko had been quiet and their relationship had been peaceful for the most part. lauren and herb had ended up getting back together shortly after she finally allowed him to explain what happened so after a long time of thinking , she decided to take him back and build on their relationship together. thought chianti and david weren't to happy with her decision, they loved her dearly and just wanted her to be happy so they kept their negative thoughts and opinions to themselves and allowed their friend to be happy.

david's face fell along with the tears before he pulled her into a big bear hug allowing her to lightly cry into her chest " what's wrong, what's your problem mama ? " he soothed.

chianti's chest heaved a couple times before she finally had the breathing space to speak " b-b-because you said I was acting crazy " chainti whined wiping her tears , lucky she didn't have on any makeup so her face just looked super puffy.

david was confused to say the least. every since a couple months ago , chainti had been overly sensitive about everything. Her attitude was already bad from the start , but know it seemed like anything made her cry.

you yelled at her ? She cried. You made a joke about her ? She cried. Her sock got wet from an ice cube in the floor ? She cried.

even chainti didn't know why everything was suck a big deal now , all she knew was that she was said and certain things just made her cry now.

" girl I was joking " David low key laughed but still soothed her , rubbing her in back as they both stood in the middle of Zara. Staff members secretly walked past watching the couple's emotional moment but decided to leave it alone. " I still love you girl " he smiled down at her , licking his lips at her fresh face.

" no , cause now I'd not like you ... eat my ass " she rolled her eyes , pushing him off of her bow not feeling like being touched.

" girl whatever, aye ain't you supposed to be meeting' wit Lauren at three ? " david asked getting a nod of conformation from chainti. He took out his phone to look at the time seeing that it read 2:54.

" well it's two fifty-four sooo " David let her know. She whipper her head around to look to him before looking at her phone to make sure David wasn't joking around with her. She made a face before tucking her phone back into her purse and looking

" well shiet " the stood in silence while Chianti thought about what her next move would be , if she wanted to just tell Lauren to meet them at the house or if she just wanted to just cancel and spend the rest of the day with David.

" com'on you gotta drop me to the nail salon " Chianti smiled , grabbing David's arm and dragging him out of the store. The two then walked the their car , David I'm the front seat and Chianti in the passenger, music blasting threw the vehicle.

Meanwhile , emiko sat outside of her new home on her porch sipping a class of wine. Emiko had been doing alright ever since the miscarriage. However , the pstd of what happened that day with the doctor , who name and found out to me Brianna stone had been eating her alive.

apparently, the woman she had murdered was a mother of three , she was also very loved within the community she lived in. Her body had been found an hour after emiko had left when a fellow nurse walked in to check on Brianna since she hadn't left the room in a while. Which was where she was found dead.

After a while emiko had somewhat forgotten about her , until the woman at the front desk got called in for question and described her face in grave detail. A image from security camera's and from a skilled drawing was plastered all over the news in social media. So she was then forced to go on the run.

She had ran from New York to Mexico and was now residing in Miami , she had been their for a couple weeks and was now finally beginning to feel safe. She closed her eyes relaxing, feeling like she finally found peace in herself when the blaring noise of police sirens jolted her awake.

In the distance, three cop cars entered wildly into her drive way , her neighbors peaking out of their windows to see emiko sigh put her glass of wine on the side deck table , and slowly get up from the rocking chair , her hands in the air as she slowly but surely made her way down the porch steps.

a pale male coo opened up his car door , ducking in between the crack of it. His gun drawn directly at the young woman she he screamed directions at her.

" get your ass on the ground now ! " he yelled motioning to the ground with his gun. Emiko slowly pulled herself to the ground , then putting her two hands behind her head. A female cop them quickly came up behind her , roughly slamming her into the hood of the cop car where handcuffs where then put in her wrist.

" yo ass ain't never seein' the late of day again " the female cop whispered in her ear smirking at the curvy young woman. Emiko said nothing in return, just kept a stone face as blog-gers and news photographers finally showed up to the scene, thinking they where taking pictures of the young woman that had taken a loved human away from everyone until the police officer said

" emiko ronad , you are arrested for the murder of ▨▨▨▨▨ ▨▨▨▨▨▨▨ ▨▨▨. "

LeT me TaKe y'aLL BaCK

" so are you gonna help me or not ? " emiko was now back at Emily's house singing to same tune she always did. After emptying her guts about killing the woman at the doctors office and her miscarrying, the only thing on her mind was taking down Chianti and her relationship.

" emiko... you just told me that you killed a woman. AND THE ONLY THING ON YOUR MIND IS RUINING THIER RELA-TIONSHIP?! " Emily yelled paseing a whole in her floor. Emiko sat thier still quiet waiting for an answer from Emily

" what else is their to do emiko ? At this point your just trying to hard " Emily shook her head at the psychotic human being standing in front of her. Emily was truly terrified, not of emiko , but of conscience. She wasn't trying to get locked up. Besides she was already on to the neck man.

" so when you was chasing him in school that wasn't trying to hard " emiko fired back tilting her head to the side in an questioning manner. Emily sucked her teeth in response.

" listen .. I'm not going back and forth with you anymore. Emiko I'm done being a bitter bitch. That's not somethin' I'm tryna past down to my future kids okay ? Yes I fucked up in my past on SO many levels , but I know have a boyfriend, some-one that I really care about " Emily expressed, she wanted emiko to be just as happy as she now was. She finally was learning to love herself

She had now got the but surgery removed so her normal body was now back. She started focusing on her education , she had moved to another home and was now thriving along with a special someone she had met a couples months ago.

" but if it was you you'd try EVERYTHING to break them up ! Your a selfish bitch ! " emiko yelled pushing Emily. She stumbled back catching herself on the arm of her new couch before taking a deep breath and shaking her head. She then realized she couldn't help her friend because her friend didn't want to help herself.

" emiko , I'm not going to fight you. If you don't want to Listen and take accountability and reflect on your past actions.. than you need to leaves I refuse to argue with you " she ended the conversation leaving emiko in her Living room , walking out of sight into her bedroom.

Emily grabbed her phone to send a text to her boyfriend to grab a bottle of wine for the two before he made his way over to the apartment when a burning sensation filled her neck. she looked up into the mirror gasping for air when she saw emiko staring back at her , a scalpel in her hand that was plunged into her neck. the two made their way the ground as Emily lost her balance, emiko pulled the blood stained weapon out of Emily's neck before running out of the apartment, leaving the front door wide open.

is it a crime

Chianti sprayed on her nyx all nighter setting spray. She flattened out her grey dress, then turned around looking at her ass in the big mirror.

she smiled in satisfaction letting her hands move down to her flat stomach, smiling at the news her and david had found out three weeks ago.

chianti had been feeling sick for a while and had no energy to do anything. after a few days of going back and forth with herself she decided to say fuck it and went to the clinic while david was playing basketball with his younger cousin. she then found out she was five weeks pregnant.

though she was scared, david and her were nervous but excited. david immediately started reading parenting books, looking at things for the nursery, talking to her stomach while she slept. there was no doubt he was 100% ready for a child and strangely enough, chianti was aswell.

" gawd damn " chianti turned around smiling , looking at david leaning against the door frame licking his lips at the sight of his lover. he stared at her intently taking in her outfit and makeup.

" boyyy you wanna be me so bad " chianti rolled her eyes seeing that david was wearing all black just like her. He wore a black puffer jacket with a regular Hanes white t-shirt , paired with a pair of black jeans and all white air force ones. he then obviously his braids hadn't been done yet so they weren't fucked up but they were slightly ruffled , so he decided to wear a grey

" aight , you ready baby " david asked looking in the mirror at himself , fixing his chains and checking out his beard growth. chianti had put him onto Mielle hair growth oil for his patchy parts in his beard a couple weeks ago and he had been using it every night before they slept ever since.

" yea , let's go " chianti checked her lipstick one more time before grabbing her favorite black chanel bag , grabbing her house keys and made her way out the front door , david following behind her.

david held chianti by her waist , his head in her neck taking in her scent while she laughed making her way to the front counter where a pretty woman around their age stood.

" hello welc- " the women's smile dropped from her face when she saw the two. more importantly , david , and how different he looked from before.

"welcome I'm sorry" she nervously laughed secretly staring at david who was way more preoccupied sniffing chianti's perfume from her neck.

" it's fine , umm can we get a hamburger with lettuce , tomato , fried onions , mayo and ketchup and a side of onion rings please " chianti ordered turning her head around to david to order.

" uhh , lemme get the same thing " he ordered. The woman nodded letting her now that the food would be brought out to them and the both walked towards a booth near the window.

chianti pulled out her phone and scrolled threw instagram since she hadn't gotten a chance to do so throughout the day while david smiled staring at her. chianti looked up slowly at david who was staring back at her with a smirk on his face.

"watchu lookin' at papa ? " chianti softly spoke , setting her phone down on the table smiling at him.

" you so sexy. " he replied biting his lip leaving butterflies to erupt in chianti's stomach. the woman watched from afar, her stomach in knots of jealousy. her eyes burned with rage as she spoke to herself while preparing the couples food.

" I can't believe he didn't notice me - " she shook her head in disbelief and confusion. " I guess he really did move on " she said to herself, grabbing the food and putting it in the serving tray , quickly mentally gathering herself and making her way to the couples table.

" here's you food , hope you guys enjoy " the woman put on a fake happy voice sitting the meals down on the table , then leaving back to her station at the front of the restaurant.

the two started to dig into their meals leaving the table in silence , nothing but the sounds of chianti's happy humming. david ate his food , sneaking glances at his woman in awe watching her dance lightly in her seat.

he laughed shaking his head , then leaned back putting his back onto the booth and rubbing his fingers together in a circular motion to get the crumbs from the burger off of his hands.

" so i was thinkin' - " david started, stoping for a moment to take a sip of his water. " we need to get anotha' home. especially since we adding somebody else to the team " david said referring to the infant growing inside of chianti.

" you sure ? I mean that's gon' be a little expensive " chianti made a face thinking if the cost of the home and furniture.

" don't een worry about allat. I got y'all aight ? just focus on staying healthy and ignoring all negative shit. " david waved her off picking an onion ring off chianti's place.

" mmtch. okay , but I call dibs on paying for the furniture " chianti smiled knowing there was nothing that could be said by david to stop her from buying ever piece of furniture in their new home.

" aight fine " david agreed taking another bite of his burger.

" aight now I want a milkshake " chianti sighed , full from the food she had just ate rubbing her stomach. david sucked his teeth giving her a knowing look,

" now mama. you know you lactose and some shit " david reminded her. he watched as chianti purposely ignored his comment as she flagged down the woman standing behind the register causing the woman to nervously make her way over to the too

" hey.. is everything okay ? are you guys ready for the bill ? " the woman spoke a hundred miles a minute confusing chianti.

" uhhh , yea but can I also get a milkshake to go ? can you make it cookies and cream ? " chianti ordered , watching the woman quickly gather the left over food off the trays.

" um okay ! I'll be back with that and with the check , bye ! " she replied quickly walking away , stepping over her own to feet.

" she reallll nervous " chianti acknowledged getting the attention of david who shook his head.

" yea , that's my weird ass ex , I'm apologize for not telling you when we first walked in. I just ain' wanna have her say sum' slick shut and she end up tryna fight you , cause then imma go to jail " david explained in the most serious tone he could come up with shrugging.

" oh okay , I'm not really worried bout it though. as long as we locked in ain' no bitch gon make me sweat "chianti stated , swiping her hand under her chin in the 'period' motion.

" damn right " david tried to make his voice sound girly causing chianti to laugh as they both leaned in for a kiss.

the acoustic version of kill bill played throughout the car as the young woman cried scrolling threw her phone at the pictures of her and david.

zyon and david dated from their junior year of highschool to their freshman year of college. the two's relationship was very toxic , the two were truly only dating because of the popularity they got from dating eachother. but a couple weeks before the end of freshman year , a scandal had invaded the school of a sex tape with zyon and another man at the school.

the video had him viral everywhere , it was on twitter porn pages , she was getting asked out left and right from dudes at their school after they saw how much of a 'freak' she was and a little while after that , david had broke up with her and cut her off completely.

it felt like the breakup was just hitting her, she had thought she was fine since it had happened ariunf three years ago. but seeing him with another girl , watching him admire her , kiss on her , giving her everything that she could've had made her blood run cold.

zyon sighed , her thumbs dancing across her phone screen before she finally thought 'fuck it' and clicked the message button on david's Instagram profile.

" it's worth a shot " she mumbled to herself before sending him a small text.

she sat her phone down in her lap watching the door of the restaurant as the couple walked out , david's hand wrapped around chianti's shoulder as they laughed about something that was said by one of them.

she then watched as david pulled out his phone and read something causing something in zyon's mind to let her know it was the dm she had just sent. she almost felt her heart-strings pull as she watched him shake his head and show chianti whatever was on her phone.

chianti laughed lightly at what was on the phone before taking his phone and putting it in her purse. zyon scoffed in jealousy at the action of chianti before aggressively putting her car into drive and skrtting off in her car with david in her mind heavy.

IT'S a wrap

David listened to chianti continue to vent as they drive on the freeway towards his mothers house. ever since they left the restaurant she had been on one. some girls would call her insecure or say that she was adding life to it by speaking on it , it ti her it was more about respect. if you clearly see your ex with his new girlfriend who's pregnant, why would your first course of action be to dm him ? ghetto.

" I swear that bitch really tried it. she lucky I'm pregnant or I'd do that hoe like persuasion and slump her ass in a sink " chianti finished her rant , rubbing her stomach to calm herself.

though as many times as she told herself she didn't want kids and she would never want kids , it was just something about knowing that she would be a mother in a couple months that changed her whole aspect on motherhood.

by the time she had finally calmed herself down , they were pulling up in david's mother's driveway. chianti looked at the exterior of the home in amazement at how beautiful the molding was , her mouth agap and her hand in her stomach as always

"girl come on "david chuckled at her facial expression while he held the door for her , his hand out to help her while she stepped out of the vehicle.

david balled his right hand into a fist and knocked on the front door , creating a beat until he heard his mothers heavy footsteps coming towards the front door from inside the home.

"who in the hell - "his mother snatched the from door open , her face balled up until she saw chianti. her mug changed quickly into a excited smile as she practically jumped onto chianti giving her the biggest hug of life.

"OMG MY DAUGHTA' IN LAW ! "cookie pulled her out of the hug to take a good look at her , she took a note of the small hard feeling she received from the lower part of her stomach.

"COME ON GIRL ! I just made some of my special Indian street tacos "cookie bring her shoulders up in excitement bringing chianti towards the kitchen , leaving david in the fore.

"damn mamma , I thought I was your favorite son "david pouted jokingly dragging his feet towards the kitchen where the two woman sat talking at the breakfast bar.

" boy shush , you my only son " cookie lightly smacked david in the back of his head , rolling her eyes at how dramatic he could be

every since david was young he was always a momma's boy but not in a weird way that most are. his mother made sure to teach him how to treat a woman when he got old enough to be with one. she always wanted him to be better than his father , she always wanted him to create a family of his own.

she made sure to let him know that no women is be dis-respected without reason , how to take rejection , how to communicate and many other things to help him when he became a man.

" anyways , ms.brewster - " chianti started but was cut off my cookies hand being put in her mouth.

" un uh , girl what I tell you bout' calling me that ? " cookie started , her head leaned back " I told you ms.brewster is only for people I don't know , and don't like , like that bitch emily " cookie mummered at the end getting a chuckle from chianti.

" my apologies mamma , but we have something to tell you - " chianti grabbed her hands for support getting up from her seat on the bar stool. " we're pregnant! " chianti announced.

" OH MY GOD ! " the older woamn yelled as she started clap-ping in excitement and kissing chianti's cheeks repeatedly.

" ouuu I gotta start planning right now , shit I gotta call my florist, then I gotta call aunt mary and tell her to put everybody , EXCEPT THAT BITCH RONNY on the invite list , damn lemme call porsha and tell her to clear my schedule for the rest of the day " cookie started to rant then grabbed her phone and started to dial porsha's number.

" well I guess we don't have to ask you if you wanna plan everything " david and chianti chuckled at how quick his mother jumped on planning the baby shower and gender reveal.

" aight now I love y'all , but y'all gotta get up on outta here , I got a whole bunch of ordering and planning to do " cookie shoo'ed the young couple out of her home as they laughed heading to front door with cookie following close behind them.

" alright now y'all be good fa me , I'll see y'all later and chianti text me your next appointment! " cookie gave her final goodbyes before blowing a kiss to the couple and heading back inside her home.

cookie let the door close and stood there before happy tears started to run down her face. she looked around her home at everything she needed to baby proof before laughing to herself

" cookie ... you about to be a grandma " cookie spoke to herself smiling.

☒☒☒☒☒☒ ☒☒☒☒☒☒ ☒☒☒☒

☒☒☒☒☒☒☒☒ , ☒:☒☒ ☒☒

☒☒☒ ☒☒☒☒ | ☒☒☒☒☒

lauren blankly stared at herb threw the salon mirror as he sat in the corner , his eyes glued to whatever was on his phone. she played with her hands , something that she did when she was when she was nervous or her gut was telling her something she was trying to ignore.

she looked she looked at her hairstylist, an older woman that had been doing her hair since she was in highschool and the older woman gave her a knowing lips popping her gum , before shaking her head and looking back down at her hands as she flatironed her hair

" you glued to your phone. " she flatly said looking at him through the mirror. her words caused herb to stop his actions of liking on of the many girls he followed on instagram to look up at his girlfriend.

" what else am I supposed to do when you getting to hair done , I'm bored as fuck lauren. " he said staring at her in annoyance. lauren sat staring at him for a moment before nodding.

herb let out a breath he had no idea he was holding and decided to watch his girlfriend while she got her hair done.

for the first couple months of lauren and herb getting back together things were amazing. he was under her twenty four seven , he started considering her feelings , he even gave her his pass word and she was check his phone almost all the time. but soon enough things went right back to normal , and since he was Lauren's first and only relationship, she took it.

mostly because he was all she was used too but also because he had made her so insecure that she was scared to be alone. she was so used to him and his ways that she felt like she would never find better.

the front door to the salon opened causing a tiny alarm sounds to go off, herb looked at the door and felt his stomach drop to his ass.

" daquan I swear if you don't pay for my hair imma key yo car again ! " a woman , who's name was Lina yelled into her phone facing the window

oh my fucking lord . Why me ?! , I don't see this bitch no where else in up public, now all of a sudden I see that bitch after I fucked the shit outta her not but three days ago ?! Herb thought to himself, his heart beating out of his chest.

A couple nights ago , herb cheated on lauren with a woman he met at the club , Lina. he thought that it would be his last time seeing it speaking to her but here we are , his girlfriend and side bitch both in the same salon together.

" baby imma be back I gotta go pay real quick " lauren informed as she grabbed her wallet out of her purse and followed her hair dresser to the back.

herb and Lina sat in a few seconds of silence before a smirk graced her face and she made her way towards the seat lauren was just sitting in that was located right in front of herb.

" heyyy " she dragged smiling at him which he didn't respond to , his eyes glued to his phone.

" damn can't speak ? "

" what's good ? " he mumbled , quickly looking at the door lauren just walked into to make sure she wasn't watching what was happening, the back at Lina.

" shit yo dick is - " she began giggling " I been reminiscing bout it , I'm tryna have it in me again" she bit her lip , leaning forward and letting her hand caress his thigh.

" can you not ? " he snatched his leg from her hand , " don't talk about the shut we do in private in public " he lectured grabbing his phone that was seated next to him and stood up stretching.

" ight I'll text you then papi " she smiled , then got back on her phone smirking when she saw her baby father sent her some money to get her hair done.

" ight bet " he smiled but dropped it and looked the other way when he heard Laurens laughter as she walked up to herb

" alright I'm done , you like it ? " she smiled asking , doing a 360as her bundles flowed down her back.

" yea baby - " he nodded kissing her cheek " I love it , now let get in outta her , I'm hungry as shit " he groaned making Lauren laugh and nod as they left the store "woowww" Lina scoffed "he has a whole girl, obviously she ai t got nothin on me" she rolled her eyes "damn Lina, you taking everybody's man this year" she laughed yo herself.

this wasn't the first time this year lina had been sleeping with a taken man, but something about doing so boosted her confidence. It made her feel wanted and desired, so to see how beautiful lauren was and to know that herb, a taken man, wanted her made her confidence boost to u known degrees.

"aight food your back, I just want a peek-a-boo quick weave" lina smiled at the hairstylist who nodded and turned her around to face the mirror.

Heard It All

"I don't even know why we agreed to this shit " david shook his head , pouting like a child as he put a small coat of coco butter on his face in the bathroom.

"yeah I know - "chianti sighed from the bedroom connected to their bathroom " but we told lauren we would double date with her " chianti reminded david , who sucked his teeth coming out the bathroom applying his rings.

a couple days prior , lauren practically begged chianti and david to double date with her and herb , it took a lot of convincing but the two reluctantly said yes only for lauren's happiness.

david fell onto the bed on his back laying right next to chianti. the two sat in comfortable silence , just the occasional tiktok audios from the videos chianti was watching in her phone " you know if we call right now and say we both sick we won't have to go " david smiled.

chianti bursted into laughter at his request before getting up from the bed and making her way to their shared closet. she came out a few moments later with a pair of glossy black heels and some green slides that belonged to david , sat on the bed holding the bottom of her stomach and sat her boots down in front of her.

" you laughin , i'm being foreal. i'm not really happy with going to the dinner with that weird ass nigga all night. i swear lauren lucky she like my sister and I don't want her to be disappointed. " david ranted standing up from the bed and putting on chianti's shoes for her.

" I know baby , but we promised we'd go so " chianti shrugged. personally she didn't wanna go either but she refused to allow her friend to feel lonely on valentine's day , that was really the only thing that was stoping her from say fuck it and staying with her baby.

" aight man - " david sighed reluctantly grabbing his keys off the nightstand " let's head out " he let chianti walk out in front of him out the front door as they walked into the parking lot.

" you looking good as hell baby ! " david yelled out to chianti who wasn't walking to far in front of him causing her to look back to see he was recording her.

" boy bye " she said blushing. david jogged to stand in front of her to get a front angle of her " com'on baby. show these hoes why they can't fuck witchu ma " he gassed her.

" ahhh " she stuck her tounge out as she started to strut to the car , david hyping her up as she did so.

" aight aight I'm done " she laughed standing by the passenger seat door waiting for david who came by a few seconds later giving her a kiss and opening up the car door for her.

david jogged towards the drivers seat before getting in and starting to car. chianti connect her phone to the radio playing who can I run to by Xscape as they started their journey to the restaurant.

lauren and herb sat at the dinner table in awkward silence , Lauren checking her phone periodically and herb texting Lina under the table.

after the meeting at the salon , lina and herb had formed a relationship with one another and had been talking non stop since. herb felt no guilt whatsoever for his actions. In his eyes she would obviously allow him to continue to cheat if she took him back , so what stop ? let's just face the trust , the relationship spark wasn't there anymore.

" girllll you look bomb " lauren smiled seeing chianti walking towards her with her arms wide open for a hug and which lauren immediately ran into

" thank you sis , you look gorgeous aswell obviously period you is DEFINITELY somebody's fine mama " she gassed spinning chianti around.

" what's good sis " david greeted giving her a side hug and kissing her cheek. " hm I gotchu these since I know ole boy

didn't " david gestured towards herb sitting in the booth quiet
as a mouse.

" thank you - " she smiled " umm let's sit down and order huh
? " she smiled at the couple causing them to both nod and get
into the booth , chianti side eyeing herb as she did so.

lauren sat next to her man as the three talked while herb sat
in the corner left out , his eyes glued to his phone like always.
lauren tried sneaked little looks at herbs phone during the
dinner but she was still more into the conversation than herb.

david stared at chianti in pure bliss while she laughed with
lauren , her make up flawless done along with her long red
nails and her black curly bundles that fell done her back.

" watchu staring at boy ? " chianti softly said dragging her
hand across the back of his neck. he bit his lip at the feeling
of her acrylics touching him before grabbing her chin and
bringing her face in close to whisper in her ear.

" I hope you don't think you going to sleep when we get
home , im beatin that shit out the frame soon as we touch
down at the crib ma " david whispered licking her ear then
giving her a small cheek kiss before letting her go.

chianti's cheeks turned bright red as she let out a giggle and
looked down at her plate. meanwhile , lauren took a small sip
of her wine and looked down into herbs lap to see someone
by the name of 'pizza hut' had called him for the third time
since they'd been at dinner.

lauren slammed her wine glass down on the table and turned her head towards herb who was in a completely different world to even notice his girlfriends glare

hear we go chianti thought shaking her head and sinking into the sink , pulling out her phone and scrolling on twitter

" herb who tha fuck is that texting your phone " lauren shifted in her seat to face herb. herb's head quickly popped up from his phone and his eyes became set on his girlfriend who was already staring at him.

" man - " he sucked his teeth " it ain't nobody , just chill and enjoy the evening lauren. " he warned her. though it seemed like he was calm , his heart was beating a million miles a minute. despite how he treated lauren , he did love her and the thought of losing her again was sickening.

" obviously you do know them if they blowing up your fuckin phone like that ! on valentine's day at that ? " lauren snapped tilting her head to the side staring at herb. herb stared at her for a few seconds before shaking his head and grabbing his cup , talking a sip of his hennessy and getting back on his phone

" oh you think you funny huh ? " lauren laughed smirking at the side of his face and nodded " aight - " she snatched his phone clear out of his hands causing him to attempt lightly to fight back for it but to no avail.

chianti pushed her lips out to her nose and gave herb the side eye , then pulled out her phone and started to text david.

chianti and david both closed their phone just in time to see lauren send a powerful punch to herb shoulder leaving him slouched over into his chair in pain.

" REALLY HERBET ?! PIZZA HUT ?! YOU SAVED THE DUMB BROAD INDER PIZZA HIT ?! HOW STUPID DO YOU THINK I AM ?? " lauren yelled bringing attention of other couples and families in the restaurant while the servers just continued working and minded their business.

" bro you just assuming shi- " herbet attempted to plead his case but got met with the hardest slap across the face he had ever received.

" AIN'T NO FUCKIN' PIZZA HUT ON PLANET EARTH GON SIT UP HERE AND CALL AND TEXT YOU CALLING YOU BABY AND SHIT ITS CLEARLY A BITCH UNLESS YOU GAY " lauren snapped standing up from the table as she slammed her fist into her hand as she spoke.

" oh wow " chianti spoke giving herb a look while she rubbed her stomach and david sat in the corner of the booth holding his laugh back.

" lauren brah I don't know that bitch " herb lied trying to reach for lauren's hand causing her to snatch them back

david shook his head and pulled out his phone going back to his and chianti's text thread.

" oh you don't know her huh ? - " lauren tilted her head In question " well how about we call her right ? " lauren went to the contact ignoring Herbert's plead's and reaches for his phone.

lauren put the phone to her ear and aloud it to ring for a good w before somebody finally answered " who is this ?! " lauren put her hand on her hip.

" and who is this ? " lina sat up in her bedroom , summerwalker playing lightly on her tv as she sat in her bra and underwear.

" this is lau - ren. why the fuck you keep calling my fuckin' man ?! " lauren yelled , her finger moving all kinds of way.

" who herb ? " lina chuckled through the phone making her way to the bathroom with her phone.

" you know who the fuck im talkin' about " lauren snapped back , still holding the phone to her ear and lowering her voice.

" listen I don't know who the fuck you think you are but tell herb to call me it's important " lina sassed back stepping to the side in the bathroom mirror and going over the frame of her belly.

" you know what ? imma send you the addy you can come and tell him whatchu gotta tell him now " lauren hung up the phone with that and quickly sent lina the address causing chianti and david to gather their things , leave their part of the bill money and leave.

" WE LEAVING LAUREN PEACE OUT " chianti let her know , she wasn't trying to have to fight anybody while pregnant she knew how protective david was over her so she just decided it would be better to leave.

" bro what the fuck is you doin' ? why the fuck your tryna fight about something you don't even know about " herbet tried to make since with his explanation but only made himself sound stupid.

" im not tryna fight

her , best believe if I wanted to I would've made it known " lauren said staring at the front entrance of the restaurant waiting for the unknown woman to into the restaurant.

" man all she finna do is lie " he tried to plead his case getting a scoff from lauren.

" oh now you know how she is ? - " lauren laughed turning to look at him with her eyebrows raised " I fuckin' hate you bro " lauren shook her head , her eyes tearing up ad she walked out of her restaurant herb hit in her tail.

" listen I'm not here to start to shit or nothin " lina caught Lauren the second she stepped foot out the restaurant , she recognized her face from herbs lock screen " I just wanted to let you know herb , im pregnant and it's yours " silence rang out between the three while Lauren's started to burn from more tears.

" I didn't wanna do it like this but you been ignoring me so " lina shrugged without a care in the world.

" wow. " lauren scoffed before pushing herb as herb as hard as she could " FUCK YOU HERB. I WANTED A BABY WITH YOU

FOR FUCKIN EVER. REGARDLESS IF ITS EVEN YOURS YOU FUCKED HER WHILE YOU WAS WITH ME ?! IM SO FUCKIN DONE WITH YOU " lauren cried. she stared him in the eyes for a moment before shaking her head and walking towards her car , the car they both took to the restaurant. herb yelling her name as she got in and started her car.

" listen I don't give a fuck about y'all in stable ass

relationship. all I know is you better be ready to take care of yo kid " lina said before strutting back to her car leaving herbet in front of the restaurant. alone.

" Heard it all before (heard it all before)

Let me explain, baby, it's not what you think, that's what you said to me "

LOVING BABY BREWSTER

A b6 month later

david's hands grazed chianti's six month pregnant stomach as he spread a handful of coconut oil on her stomach. chianti rubbed his head through his durag as she smiled down at him while his eyes stayed laser focus on her stomach while he watched the small movements poke out of her stomach.

" you ready for today ? " david looked up at chianti's chunky face smiling back down at her. since last month , chianti's face had became a lot chunkier especially her nose. when she first realized she tried to hide it for as long as she could , she stoped posting everywhere except twitter and still hadn't posted her pregnancy at all.

" duhh , I'm so excited I swear I'm jumping for joy on the inside but I can't cause ya daughta' weighing me down " chianti lightly bounced on the edge of the bed. they both swore up and down that they were having a daughter even though they had no proof because patrice was like a vault when it came to the gender , they both just had a feeling it was a girl.

" I'm only sliiightly nervous because we invited lauren and herbet " chianti rolled her eyes at the mention of her best-friends 'lover' as did david.

" ion even know why she still wit dude , but I mean hey that yo friend you needa' help her out. " david threw his hands up in defense , pushing his lips upward towards his nose

" you right but I mean hey - " she shrugged " you can't help somebody that don't wanna be helped , I'm not bout to keep wasting my time to help her , have all these conversations about her being better than that with her , helping her move all her stuff outta his house just for her to run right back to him. when she finally get's fed up then I'll try my best to help her , but until then I'm not saving nobody that don't wanna be saved " chianti finished her statement getting a head nod in response from david.

" word is bond i hope she realize her worth soon , I can't keep playin' nice wit ole boy just because i care about lil sis " david spoke. he watched while chianti got up from the side of the bed going to the closet and coming back out the a grey strapless dress on.

" yea me too - " chianti sighed " but enough about they toxic asses , lemme take my ass in this living room for armani drag me " chianti laughed wobbling her way to the kitchen.

" bitch finally ! i don' already set up everything about - " armani checked his iced out rolex " an hour ago ! and you still standing there staring at me staring at you. girl bring yo ass mommy to be " armani cursed getting laughs from both david and chianti.

" aight boo - " david kissed her lips twice " I'll see you at the venue , I gotta go get my haircut " david announced grabbing his keys off the counter as the two said their goodbyes and david made his way out the door.

chianti flattened out her white dress , smiling as she slowly rubbed over her baby bump before the sprinter came to a halt. the driver then got out of his seat and made his way to the side of the car letting her out and walking her into the building.

david's eyes scanned the room before they came to a halt as a smile quickly crept onto his face as he saw his pregnant girlfriend walking towards him. he held out his arms for a hug inviting chianti into his arms.

" you look beautiful mama " david kissed her forehead causing a smile to creep onto chianti's face. cookie stood near the food table smiling watching the couple interact, she watched as david looked into chianti's eyes with so much love and happiness.

"thank you baby , you don't like to had yourself" chianti smiled as david twirled her around in his arms.

cookie watched the two interact with a big smile on her face from the snack bar. her heart warmed as she watched the two interact just like her and her late husband , luscious would interact with on another.

"hey baby" cookie greeted walking up to chianti with open arms , welcoming the young mother into a heart warming hug.

"hey momma" chianti smiled , her chin resting on cookies shoulder. cookie pulled chianti away from the hug after a moment talking a good look at her,

"alright well the foods done so let's come on and eat " cookie announced before walking away to the dining area of the home they rented out.

"alright we'll be there " david grabbed chianti's forearm before she walked off , pulling her into a tiny corner as cookie , lauren and herb as well as the other guest trailed into the dining area.

"y'all better hurry up before everybody eat up all the food ! " cookie yelled shaking her head at the two as they smiled at eachother.

"watchu want boy I'm hungryyy" chianti smiled up at david as he did the same but looked down at her cause of the height difference between the two

" baby jus wanna love you for the rest on my life. fuck the past. fuck all the crazy shit because we both know we together for a reason , since the day we got together every moment since then to now has been put in our path as a test and until we get to our wedding i refuse to let fights and arguments keep me from putting that ring on your finger and somemo' of my kids in your stomach " david whispered in her ear before laying his head down on her chest.

chianti's heart fluttered at his speech , she loved how he was never scared to tell her how he really felt about her and wet he could make her just by his voice. she loved how he made her feel like she was the only girl on the planet he cared for.

" boy stop making me blush , I love you too though baby " she kissed him softly on his lips " com'on let's go eat this food im starving " chianti instantly got excited mentioning her food , grabbing david's hand and dragging him towards the dining area.

" girl yo ass always hungry " he laughed following behind her , his hand wrapped into hers.

" there y'all areeeee , ouuu and theirs my niece or nephew " lauren laid a light kiss and chianti's stomach getting a kick from the baby.

" what y'all hoping for " lauren question, sinking her fork into some of the mac and cheese on her plate. chianti sat back rubbing her stomach while David laid his hand back in his chair.

" all I want is a healthy baby , but david swear it's a girl " chianti rolled her eyes smiling at david.

" no. i know it's a girl " david boosted getting and glare from chainti.

" awwwww that's so cute " lauren cooed at the couple silently praying that her and herb could get their shit together and be like them one day.

" don't start that bullshit " herb murmured towards her before closing his phone and walking out of the home , slamming the door and his way out.

the room went quiet for a few moments, chianti tearing her plate up and david shaking his head at herbs actions. cookie looked at everyone seeing that nobody was going to say anything so she decided to say what needed to be said.

" umm sweetheart is that your man ? " cookie tapped Lauren pointing to the closed front door.

" unfortunately, yes " she sighed setting her head down on the table.

" mhm , well uhh you need to get with a real nigga and drop that bitch outside " cookie blurted out getting a shocked looked from and chianti.

" hey I'm just saying , but that ain't my man so who am I to argue " cookie threw her hands up In defense.

" tuh girl you said it better than I would've " kimberly , chianti's mother co-signed. the two ended up meeting during the planning of the gender reveal and became the best of friends since , they called eachother all the time.

" alright na enough about bitch boy , let's start opening some gifts " cookie announced as everyone got up from the dining table and made their way to the gift room made by cookie and kimberly.

" alright now y'all ready to find out the gender ! " cookie yelled as they all gathered around the couple. the two stood over a big painted box that had balloons the color of the baby's gender. black meaning boy and purple meaning girl.

" yessirrrr " david yelled , practically jumping for joy at this point.

" alright now ... OPEN ! " cookie yelled causing the couple too open the the box letting

   purple balloons fly out of the box.

" oh my goodddd ! " lauren yelled jumping up and down.

" I knew it ! I swea I knew it " david picked up chianti spining her around causing her to giggle. cookie , lauren and kimberly ran towards the couple bringing them into a group hug and the only thing that ran through the three woman's mind's was

   I can't wait to go shopping.

" I trade it all for you before I write my last rap when you get older, I'll tell you how I stashed packs and tucked weed in my socks and had to flee from the cops "

Here She comes

5 months later.

chianti sat on the couch of her and david's empty home as she searched on furniture website adding more things to her already filled cart. she stroked her daughters head full of hair whilst she payed for all of the items in her online cart such as a tv , coffee table and a newer couch along with a couple more kitchen utensils and supplies on amazon.

chianti smiled satisfied with her purchase as well as her life while she looked at her fiancé and her 2 month old daughter , both sleeping peacefully in their home.

everyone in their close circle were doing great in life. lauren finally got rid of herbet and now spent her days single and focusing on herself and building back up her confidence that she had lost being with him , emiko had got of prison her good behavior and had apologized to both chianti and david , she even spend close to fifty thousand dollars on the beautiful baby girl and was now in therapy to deal with her mental issues.

patrice had met herself a new man who made her happy and who david approved of aswell as chianti , chianti's parents were still doing well as they were before and lastly chianti had gotten her degree in law and was working on starting her own black women only law firm while david was being drafted to play for the phoenix suns with his close friend kevin durant.

chianti stared at their sleeping daughter kairi for a few minutes watching her breath as her tiny lips stayed in a pout. she kissed her daughters forehead and as silently as possible, she made her way up the stairs to the third door in the right wheee her daughters nursery was located.

she silently twisted the door knob and turned on the night light stars david had installed on the walls and tiptoed towards the big circle crib her and david had got her custom made two months before she was born.

kairi cooed quietly as she was laid down onto her crib cuddling up to her bulbasaur plushie as she sleeps causing her mother to softly smile at the sight. she sighs before stretching and going back down the stairs putting her macbook on the charger in the wall and laying on her sleeping fiancés chest , getting comfortable for a good nights sleep.

"i love you mama " david told his fiancé while cuddling up close to her , snuggling his face into her neck after pecking it softly. chianti giggled running her hands through her husbands hair , smiling thinking about the two years they had spent together , the good , the bad , and the ugly.

" i love you too papa " she softly replied kissing his lips before drifting off to sleep laying under her husband.

EPILOGUE

5 years later

'i see it clear, my heart is here
we got each other and let's take it from there
and if I could I'd love you a forever end time '
the man lightly leaned on his toes back and forth while watching the entrance of the venue of his wedding. he thought back on all the wonderful moments he had with the women , the people who had tried to end them and their relationship and even their beautiful young daughter that stood at the entrance waiting for her cue to start her flower girl routine.

david was snapped out of his deep thoughts by ' a couple of forevers ' being played on the piano as everyone's body's rose from the pews while his daughter and future wife walked down the isle , his daughter throwing red and whole rose petals on the floor and his while walking close behind her.

the venue

chrisette michele herself sung softly by the piano while chianti walked down the isle smiling at her husband as he watched him wipe a few tears at the beauty of his wife. his best man , de'angleo gave him a brotherly pat on his back as his wife finally made it down the long altar and the music stopped while the priest made his way towards the couple and stood before them.

"dearly beloved, you have come together into the house of the church so that in the presence

of the church's minister and the community. vour intention to enter into marriage may be strengthened by the lord with a sacred seal." the priest spoke as everybody sat back down in thief chair , kairi sitting with her grandparents swinging her legs back and forth.

" david , do you take this woman to be your wife, to live to-gether in holy matrimony, to love her, to honor her, to comfort her, and to keep her in sickness and in health, forsaking all others, for as long as you both shall live?" the priest turned his head towards david asking him. david stared at his wife for a moment , captivated by her beauty.

" i do. " he answered holding his wife's hands.

" chianti , do you take this man to be your husband, to live together in holy matrimony, to love him, to honor him, to comfort him, and to keep him in sickness and in health, forsaking all others, for as long as you both shall live?"the priest turned to chianti who stared at her husband the same way he stared at her.

" i do " she responded the exact way her husband responded before her.

" you may now recite your vows " the priest gave the couple permission.

" david , I was not expecting you, I was not even looking but some how you came to me, as if you knew what I was needing. believe it or not I tried to resist it not wanting to let this begin, I was afraid of getting close to someone and letting my heart get broken again. For some reason you were persistent and reached out to me once more, your words felt real to me but I needed to be sure. I needed to look into your eyes to see if they spoke the truth, I had to make sure my heart would be safe with you, please understand I guard it with all my worth. The moment I looked into your eyes I felt myself give way, I knew my heart was safe with you and that's where it would forever stay. Thank you for finding me and making me your own, I promise this to you my love with me you will always be at home. david , i will also promise you this, I will make sure you always feel how much I love you with every touch and kiss. thank you for loving me. " chianti gave her speech watching her husband's eyes swell up with tears by the heart felt vows his wife just told him.

" beautiful. david ? " the priest complimented turning to david.

" i gotta warn y'all mines aren't as good as her's - " he looked out into the audience of his and her family's getting a couple chuckles from them

" chianti baby , i promise to never cheat on you i promise whenever you need me just call and i'm on my way no matter what i'm doing i promise to always be there for you mentally and physically

i promise if you ever need anything money, clothes, advice, just ask and it's yours i promise to give me all in everything i do for you i promise to make sure our kids and our future will be great i promise to love you with my fullest and be completely honest with you i promise that as long as you got my back ima ride for you i promise never to betray you

i love you baby girl and don't forget this , because

i'm going to live up to every promise i just said " david ended kissing his wife's hand as she two started to cry happy tears from her husbands word's.

" beautiful words , now chianti repeat after me " the priest instructed causing chianti to nod. " i chianti, take you david , to be my husband, to have and to hold from this day forward, for better, for worse, for richer, for poorer, in sickness and in health, to love and to cherish, till death do us part." the priest spoke.

" i chianti, take you david , to be my husband, to have and to hold from this day forward, for better, for worse, for richer, for poorer, in sickness and in health, to love and to cherish, till death do us part. "chianti repeated staring directing into the eyes of her husband.

"now david, i ask you to repeat the same with the obvious changes " the priest asked watching david nod and start to recite the words.

"i david, take you chianti , to be my wife, to have and to hold from this day forward, for better, for worse, for richer, for poorer, in sickness and in health, to love and to cherish, till death do us part." david recieted as he watched lauren and de'angelo's son come down the isle with his ring while david and chianti's daughter kairi came down the isle with chianti's ring.

"I give you this ring as a token and pledge of our constant faith and abiding love." david said sliding the ring on chianti's finger as she did the same reciting his words.

" by the power vested in me and under the laws of the state of new york I know pronounce you husband and wife , you may kiss the bride "the priest spoke causing david to grab his wife and dip her , indulging in a steamy tounge kiss in front of everyone. he let her up watching a blush and giggle as their now family watched and clapped as the couple walked down the isle.

the brides maids and grooms men along with their family followed them outside to their carriage that was set to take them to a private airport to fly them he pair to bora bora for their honeymoon.

the princess in the frog inspired carriage started to move slowly away from the venue as the family waved goodbye to the pair , lauren and her boyfriend front and center. chianti then grabbed her bouquet and turned around , then threw it into the crowd of people watching lauren catch it , surprising herself and her boyfriend while chianti laughed at the expression on the two's face while their faces faded as the carriage grew further away from their family.

"we're finally alone " chainti exhaled flopping down on the carriage seats next to her husband who draped his arms over her shoulder while her leg layed on top of his.

"thank you for showing me how to truly love a person " david spoke leaving a smile on chianti's face as she leaned in and kissed him.

and as they say in the story books , the two lived happily ever after.